DESTROY A KING

STELLA ANDREWS

FREE BOOK

Sign up to my newsletter and download a free book

stellaandrews.com

DESTROY A KING

The King of Media Corp is Dexter Prince

Possessive. Dominant. Broken.
A monster in an Armani suit.

I worked under him and was so low on his radar I barely registered.

Then it all changed with one foolish lapse of judgment. I stepped into his world with killer heels and an attitude that rubbed him up the wrong way.

I angered the beast and I'm about to pay the ultimate price because this monster has claws and is about to rip me to shreds.

So, bring it on because this victim holds a secret that will bring him to his knees.

Dexter Prince is about to discover that monsters come in all shapes and sizes and sometimes they bite back.

A deliciously dark and captivating romance with so much steam and chemistry it burns.

INTRODUCTION

The series Five Kings is about five powerful men who belong to an exclusive club. There is a plot against them to bring them down and each book tells the story of the King involved.

You may want to read them in the order written, which is as follows:
1: Catch a King
2: Steal a King
3: Break a King
4: Destroy a King
5: Marry a King (Best to read this one last.)

Dark, suspenseful, hot and steamy, they are not for the faint-hearted and some scenes may shock readers. I hope you enjoy the story.

PROLOGUE

DEXTER

*S*he looks even more beautiful in death. Like an angel. Pure, innocent and so tragic, the pain claws at my heart and replaces the love that once filled it with the emptiness I deserve.

I did this.

I killed my sister.

I will never forgive myself.

I physically ache to reach and touch the porcelain skin that has turned a deathly gray. There is no life left in those eyes that have been closed to give the appearance she's just sleeping. She will never wake up. I made sure of that and the nervous glances my way tell me they feel it too. I murdered my own sister and I will burn in Hell for eternity.

"Dexter."

A brief touch to my arm reminds me I'm not alone and there are more deserving members of my family who want to pay their respects. I can't even look them in the eye knowing the grief in them was placed there by my own hand.

I move away.

As I walk from the casket, my life changes forever. Somehow, I make it through the service and I hear the cries, letting them wash over me like a wave of blood. I killed my sister and if I can do anything to make amends, it's vowing never to make the same mistake again.

From this day on, the rules I set in place must never be broken and I will make it my life's work to uphold them. I may have caused this, but the pain I will live with forever will serve as a permanent reminder never to act in a moment of rage.

Emotion led to an act of revenge that backfired in the cruelest of ways and I won't make the same mistake twice. From now on I live by emotionless control and pack my broken heart away as surplus to requirements. I won't love and I won't accept love in return. Dexter Prince may as well have died that day, it would have better if he had.

CHAPTER 1

DEXTER

FIVE YEARS LATER

*a*s intrusions go, this one is most surprising and as I look up, my heart starts racing when I see the anger in a certain man's eyes as he says tersely, "Cut the call."

I don't even question the request because I haven't got a death wish and as I do as he says, he lowers his body into the seat opposite my desk. I'm not even surprised that Helen doesn't run in after him because everyone knows to keep their distance from this man.

Ryder King, military badass and one of the most violent, deadly men, I think I have ever met and right now he looks as if he wants me dead.

"Dexter."

He seems angry which is not a good thing — for me and I try not to let the nerves show as I face him.

"What the fuck is going on?"

"I have the same question for you?"

"Regarding..."

He slides a printed sheet of paper toward me and as I look at the image in surprise, the headline tells me I'm fucked and as I read the words, I know exactly why he came.

"What's this?"

"Tomorrow's headlines, apparently."

"Since when? I didn't authorize this."

"Then maybe you can explain why it's ready to go?"

"I can't."

I lean back in my chair and tap my fingers on the desk angrily. How the fuck is this happening? Who thinks they can get away with pissing in my factory and not being caught?

I peer a little closer and see an unfamiliar name credited to the story. Holly Bryant.

I tap the name into my computer and it pulls up the details of a journalist who works in the rag I call The Globe. Their offices are in the basement of this building and I say tersely, "The reporter works here so it should be easy enough to find out how she bypassed the usual channels. I'm pretty confident we can trace this one back but what would anyone gain from this, it's just gossip?"

"Outlined in fact. Wake up, Dexter, news has been leaking from your operation for months now, and are you seriously telling me you know nothing about it because I'm not a fool?"

"I know."

I swallow hard because Ryder King is the opposite of that and I groan. "I know I surround myself with vermin most of the day? Hell, I'm the biggest one of all but my company has procedures and if they go against them, I show them the door. This woman will soon discover that first-hand if she is trying to make a name for herself at the expense of mine."

"Or she could be working for someone else. Someone who wants to bring our organization down and stands to gain a lot from it."

He is staring at me as if I'm some sort of Bond villain and I say angrily, "Stop thinking I have anything to do with that and if you seriously doubt my loyalty to this club, then we have a major problem."

I glare at him and he nods. "Understood."

"Then who is it?"

"That's what we need to find out."

Ryder looks thoughtful which is always a good thing for us and never a good thing for the person in his sight and he sighs heavily.

"The facts are revealing a picture that spells trouble for us all. The other Kings have been set up and are fighting for survival. All our secrets are compromised and being used against us."

He shakes his head and fixes me with a hard look. "Whoever is doing this knows more than we are comfortable with, so I need you to crack down on this hard and find out who is feeding information to your reporters and allowing them to bypass your system."

"But there is only one man left if you suspect someone in this organization and you are seriously deluded if you think he's doing this."

"I didn't say that."

"But you implied it."

For a moment, I stare at Ryder with despair because if this man is involved, it's the beginning of the end and nothing will change that.

Ryder shakes his head and the look in his eye should scare the shit out of me but somehow it just settles my heart. If anyone can get to the bottom of this, he can, along with his team of assassins and intelligence operations. Just imagining him not being here makes my blood run cold and he's right that the person responsible appears to know what they're doing. Take out the foundation stone and the whole thing comes crashing down, which is why they probably started with him.

This is serious shit and I need a drink so badly right now and then Ryder says darkly, "Start with the girl, we don't have long. Find out what she knows and report back. I'll set up surveillance and make sure you're covered but remember there's someone out there who wants us gone, and we need to know who, and why?"

"Should I be worried for my life right now?"

"I thought that was something you lived with, anyway."

"True, but this time it's the unknown. Shit, I could really do without this."

"Right back at you."

"How long have we got?"

"Two weeks is my uneducated guess."

"Why two weeks?"

"Because in case you've forgotten, in two weeks the Five Kings will be united in one place for the first time in history and I'm guessing this has all been centered around that. If the person responsible wants their plan to succeed it will make sense it happens then."

"The wedding."

Ryder nods and I lean back and say gruffly, "Fuck."

He growls, "You have the ball, now it's up to you to carry it over the line. Keep in touch and do what you do best. Stick your nose in business and sniff out the story, I have every faith in you, Dexter, don't let us down."

He stands to leave and I feel like a drowning man being pulled under by an unknown force. Sort this shit out – where do I begin?

He heads toward the door and then turns and I don't miss the steely glint in his eye as he says darkly, "I don't need to remind you how important your success is. Whoever is doing this is always one step ahead of us. I have removed Hunter for his own protection but it's only a matter of time before he's compromised. He has protection but until we get to the bottom of this none of us are safe. It's time to step up, Dexter and do what you are paid extremely well to do."

"Easy enough for you to say. You can trust the men working for you, mine are all in it for their own glorification and I wouldn't trust any of them as far as I can piss in the sand."

"Then keep your enemies close and never turn your back, just know I'll be watching yours while you do what you must to end this shit."

Ryder stops and picks up a framed photograph from the table just inside my office door and I see a rare smile ghost his lips. "You know, she wouldn't want you to be this miserable."

I feel a tightness enter my chest as he reminds me of the last time I failed and I wonder if it's intentional. I doubt it because he knows how close I came to destruction at my lowest point and I shrug.

"I've learned a lot since then, I'm not the same man I was."

For some reason, I think he's almost concerned as he studies me with a hard unyielding look. Then he says harshly, "Stop blaming yourself for something you had no way of knowing. Just make it count."

I say nothing and he replaces the frame and leaves, the words hanging in the air as both a threat and a promise. Make it count. I haven't stopped trying and I'm tired of it all.

My gaze flicks to the frame and my chest tightens at the memory of a time I got things so badly wrong. If anything, it hardens my resolve and my thoughts turn to the journalist responsible for setting up this visit in the first place.

Holly Bryant isn't going to know what hit her because by the time I finish with her, she's going to wish she never set foot inside my world.

CHAPTER 2

HOLLY

*T*oday is going to be a good day. There's a spring in my step that proves to me that miracles do happen and if you work hard in life, you get everything you ever wanted.

"Morning, Holly."

I smile at Pearl, the cleaner who usually passes me on my way into the office. I always get here impossibly early because I'm desperate to succeed. To haul myself to the top of my profession and run my own publication. I am ambitious and I don't care who knows it.

It's a shame I'm just a nobody, though. A junior reporter on a gossip-led publication that ends up lining animal cages but everyone has to start somewhere and my sight is set on a greater prize than this. I want the serious news-sheet. The one they all want. The jewel in the crown and I intend on wearing it because serious hard-hitting news is in my future and I will do whatever I can to make it mine.

I waste no time and fire up the computer and check my list of things to do for today.

It must be two hours later that the office starts filling up and as the alarm buzzes on my phone, I sigh and push the serious work away because *he* will be in soon and require his usual coffee. They all will, and so I drag myself from my chair and head toward the kitchen to fetch it for them.

Yes, I'm not there yet because I'm on the first rung of the ladder and everyone knows to get to the top, you must start at the bottom first.

"Hey, gorgeous."

I nod curtly at a man who makes my flesh creep. Wayne Dawson. The seriously creepy hack who has made it his mission to add my name to the notches on his bedpost. I'm surprised there's any room left to be honest because he is a serious fuck boy and grew up into an even more vociferous player. It helps that he's good looking in a frat boy kind of way. Long floppy hair that some find endearing. Bright blue eyes that smolder when they fix on you and a boyish charm that has women shedding their panties and spreading their legs if he even looks at them in a certain way.

Not me. Maybe that's why he tries so hard, because he can't comprehend that one female in existence can't stand the sight of him.

"Wayne."

I grit my teeth as he leans against the doorjamb and runs those eyes the length of me, making me wish I'd chosen to wear a longer skirt and a looser fitting top.

He actually licks his lips as he says huskily, "Fancy grabbing a drink after work."

"I'm busy."

I keep my answer short and sweet hoping he'll get the message but he never does and as he inches closer, the small space suddenly loses all its air in a matter of seconds as he stands too close for comfort and whispers, "Then cancel."

"Can't." The kettle adds to the steam in the room and as I

pour the scalding water into the various mugs waiting, I resist the urge to throw some in his general direction.

I swear I can feel his erection pressing against my ass, and I grit my teeth and move slightly away to create distance. Counting to ten in my mind, I carry on with my job because I'm not indispensable yet, not like him and if I make a scene, it will be my head on the chopping block.

His overpowering aftershave assaults my senses and he presses in closer and whispers, "Then lunch. I could request your assistance on the interview I have set up in town. We could take five and get to know one another. What do you say?"

"I'm busy."

Once again, I keep my answer short and bitter and he growls, "You know, I could make your job a lot easier if you only let me. Keep turning me down and you'll be making coffee for the next ten years. Be a little friendlier and it will get you what you want faster, if you know what I mean."

Taking a deep breath, I say tightly, "No, what do you mean, Wayne? I'd love you to spell it out."

His breath wafts across my ear and I shiver inside as he drawls, "You make it good for me and I return the favor. We could have a lot of fun, and the only thing standing in our way is *you*."

Grabbing the tray, I turn, making him step back as it hits him in the chest and I smile brightly. "Thanks for the offer, Wayne, but as I said before, I'm busy. I'm shadowing Alyson today. We have a story to follow up at the mayor's office so maybe next time."

He nods and stands aside and as I pass, he leans down and whispers, "I'll have a word with Ray. Arrange it so you shadow me tomorrow. Dress to impress and it could be the start of something mutually beneficial."

His gaze lingers on my chest and his meaning is clear. I feel so dirty and violated as he undresses me with his eyes and, for the millionth time, wish nature hadn't been so generous when she handed out curves. My breasts have their own postal address and appear to be the stuff of every man's dreams, and I have spent most of my adult life with their eyes firmly fixed on them rather than me. It makes me sick and determined to prove I'm more than just a body and as I head off, I hate the fact I was born this way. How I wish I blended into the background wearing high neck sweaters covering a flat chest. Being short means I must wear ridiculously high heels to look my peers in the eye and, paired with my impossibly large breasts, it's a recipe for every creep out there to hit on me.

I try desperately to play it down by pulling my long, dark hair into a tight bun and wearing clothes to disguise my shape. The trouble is, they make me look like a sumo wrestler, so I gave in and dressed in a way they would expect. Sharp crisp shirt teamed with a fitted skirt and jacket. The uniform of success and yet it appears the only things they are interested in are my enlarged assets.

Well, after today perhaps they'll start taking me more seriously because the story I submitted is liquid gold and I can't wait to see it hit the wires.

CHAPTER 3

HOLLY

*I*t appears that news travels fast because as I make my way through the already busy office, there's an excitement building that's unusual. Whispered conversations over computer screens and nervous glances make me wonder what I missed. I've only been gone ten minutes and I've walked into a nervous ball of energy that wasn't there a short time ago.

The coffee is taken without a look in my direction. No thanks, no smile, just an understanding it's my job and I feel invisible most of the time because these reporters are just like me—ambitious.

I don't have the courage to ask what's happening because any words I speak may as well be background noise for all the attention they get. Yes, I'm on the bottom rung of the ladder and nobody is in a hurry to let me pass.

I make it to Ray's office and pull myself up straighter. Nobody else matters but him because he is the key to my future and is the only man I need to impress, so I fix a smile on my face and tap lightly on the door.

"What?"

He sounds angry, fearful even, and a cold feeling washes over me as I step inside the room, sensing change in the air.

I approach his desk, but his attention is firmly fixed on the monitor on his desk and he doesn't even acknowledge my presence as I set the mug down on the coaster that tells everyone he's the boss.

I hover awkwardly as if waiting for words of thanks, maybe even an explanation of what's happening, but all I get is air and so, with a sigh, I turn to the door and head outside.

The office is always busy, that kind of comes with the territory, but today there's a nervousness that I can't place and I even see Wayne whispering earnestly in the corner with his colleague Mason and whatever they're saying, it's not good news.

Taking to my desk, I glance at my own computer screen and see the reason for the madness staring me right in the face.

For some reason, my heart starts beating even faster and I feel the sweat dripping down my back as I stare at the email that has circulated among the entire staff.

Staff meeting at 10 am. All staff to attend. Dexter Prince has an announcement to make.

Unlike my peers, a shiver of excitement passes through my veins because I sense change.

Dexter Prince is coming here.

In all the time I've worked for him, I've never actually met him and for the most part, have never wanted to.

Even his name invokes fear and casts a shadow over the day. They whisper his name and tremble in their shoes at the thought he may even look in their general direction.

The man in charge. The playboy owner of Media Corp and a man who resides in his ivory tower and invokes fear in his employees.

His temper is legendary and his reach impressive and no other media organization can hold a candle to him. He is the best and deserves to sit on his throne as the biggest bastard of them all and rather than feel afraid, I am now more excited than I have ever been in my life. Bring it on because I can't wait to see perfection at its most raw, its most gritty and finally meet the man who has inspired me since I first decided I wanted a career in journalism.

It takes all my concentration to get through the next hour. Alyson stops by my desk and whispers, "Change of plan, we leave at eleven after the meeting. I must say I'm nervous. Do you think our jobs are on the line?"

I look up in surprise because somebody here is actually asking what I think and I'm so taken aback, I just stare at her for a moment as she bites her nails that have never been allowed to grow past the tip, and looks as if she's about to hyperventilate.

"Do you?"

I keep my voice steady and she shrugs. "Who knows, but I swear something's going down because that man doesn't just visit on a whim. Something's happened and it may cost us our livelihood. Maybe he's replacing us with technology or something. I wouldn't be surprised."

Resisting the urge to roll my eyes, I'm guessing Alyson was a graduate of Wayne's career progression program because she certainly fits the mold. Blue-eyed blonde with a stick thin body and no morals whatsoever. Rumor has it, she even spread them for Ray, which is how she got to be a reporter in charge of local affairs. Ironic really, when he's a married man. Having spent time shadowing her moves, I'm under no illusion she got where she is by hard work and a knack for a story. A high school graduate could write a better piece than her and it makes my blood boil when I think of the easy hall pass girls like her get, while the rest of us struggle to even get noticed.

She shrugs and turns her attention to the next group of people and as they huddle in the corner with their heads bent, once again I feel increasingly out of the loop. I know I don't play the game. I won't lower myself to their level and do what's expected. I don't gossip, and I don't join them on their drug-fueled binges on Friday night after work.

I work. Period.

I resist the office gossip and I don't make small talk. I am driven by a hunger I can't explain and I crave success, recognition and a glowing career that wins me awards and cements my future as a premier journalist admired by everyone. Which is why I struggle to move past the bottom rung, because it appears the only way up is to lower your standards and abandon your principles.

Briefly, I wonder if the story I submitted has rocked the boat a little. I took a chance and wrote an article that nobody asked me to. I had some information that I ran with and let it fly. I wonder if it landed on the wrong desk and yet far from feeling worried about that, I hope it did because the only way I will get anywhere here is by taking a chance. That's why I submitted an explosive piece that would rival any breaking scandal that will keep the wires buzzing for weeks.

Hunter Blake. The King of Wall Street is struggling, and that alone is news in itself, but when I was passed some information on his current love interest, it made for interesting reading. Lexi Mackenzie, trailer trash made good and word is she definitely spread her legs to get where she is now. Riding Hunter Blake to the finish and propelling herself up the ladder on a rocket ship.

Part of me felt bad for ripping her reputation to shreds and blaming her for Hunter Blake's fall from grace, but I'm a journalist and deal with facts that are dressed up to sell news subscriptions and go viral. I had some powerful intelligence and rather than run it by Ray, I took a chance and pressed 'send' in one rash moment of destiny.

I doubt it's the reason the great man himself is paying us a visit because that just doesn't make sense, so it must be something way bigger than that and the reporter in me is sharpening her pencil and turning to a clean page in her notebook because 10 am can't come quickly enough for me.

CHAPTER 4

HOLLY

*L*ike a storm approaching, the room waits in nervous anticipation for the man in charge to arrive. I don't think anyone can form a conversation right now as we wait with a mixture of apprehension and excitement to take our first glimpse of a man who sets himself apart from the rest of us, surrounded by an aura of notoriety and menace. Dexter Prince is an enigma. A man without character because he lets no one in to assess what that is.

I am so excited I can only focus on one thing. The door because I don't want to miss a second of the time I have to feast my eyes upon a legend.

Ray is nervous beyond belief. He is sweating and our usual fearless leader looks as if he's a hunter's prey waiting for the kill. Even Wayne has lost his cocky manner and is staring at his phone as if the answer lies on the small computer screen.

Alyson has applied a fresh smearing of lipstick and brushed her hair so it gleams like spun gold around her shoulders and I swear she's even hitched up her skirt a little to show an obscene amount of leg. The air is super-charged with a mixture of fear and desire to meet the man who pays our wages but has absolutely nothing to do with us outside of that.

The clock strikes the tenth hour and all eyes swivel to the entrance the king will enter through.

You could hear a pin drop as the door pushes open on the stroke of the hour and the sweat runs down my spine as I stare with interest at the man who enters the room like an approaching storm.

Dexter Prince is worthy of his reputation on sight.

Tall, dark and menacing, a monster dressed in an Armani suit. The cut of it reminds us all how successful he is. Darkest black to match his close-cropped hair. A black silk shirt that reinforces the image and gleaming black shoes, undoubtedly from the finest shoemaker.

A force among men - a God.

His expensive watch shines as the sunlight catches it and his dark brown eyes glance around the room with a look that could draw the secrets from the souls of every living person here. I say living because it wouldn't surprise me if some of us had died already because the dense choking toxic air that man brings with him would shrivel a person's soul in a matter of seconds.

He is not alone.

Flanking him on either side is a wall of menace. Two brutes with shaven heads and dark designer suits, much like their bosses, stand and survey the room with steely gazes. There are no smiles, no warm greeting, just a sense that we are all about to lose something valuable when he speaks.

"Holly Bryant."

I swallow—hard.

His voice is curt and irritated. Slightly husky, with a rough edge that makes me strangely weak at the knees.

All eyes turn to me and I feel the invisible arrows pointing at me as every person here breathes a sigh of relief and pushes me forward as the sacrifice, because from the look on this man's face, that's exactly what's going to happen.

The silence swirls around me as I stand on shaky legs and stare at him with a blank look that hides the terror I feel right now.

"Sir."

I look him directly in the eye and even from across the room, I feel those dark, sexy eyes, boring deep into my soul.

"Come here."

Nobody says a word and I will my legs to move because I'm more likely to run like hell the other way. Instead, I walk with a bravery that reminds me what a fucking joke I am because there is nothing good about what's coming from the look in his eye. He is angry, that's as obvious as the shit I'm obviously covered in right now and as I move to the front, he addresses the room.

"For future reference, if anyone here thinks they can play by their own rules, disregard those set in place and try to make a name for themselves at my expense, this is what happens."

My heart sinks as my hot story comes back to burn me and as I reach the front, he sneers. "Holly Bryant, you're fired."

I refuse to let the emotion show as I feel the pity surround me and yet relief that I'm the one standing here and not one of them. Even Ray has no words as he stares in disbelief at a scene none of us expected to see today—if ever.

The men beside Dexter Prince stare at me as if they're about to rip me apart limb from limb and as Dexter turns and leaves the room, they settle by my side, taking an arm each to physically escort me from the building. As experiences go, this is the most humiliating one of my life because it was so brutal, so public, and so damaging in every way.

Now I will always be that girl who was named and shamed in front of the entire staff before being dragged from the building.

I'm not even sure how I manage to put one foot in front of the other and as I walk, an increasing build-up of anger powers me on. The tears that burn are angry ones because how bloody dare he humiliate me like that. It's inhuman, *he's* inhuman and I have never hated anyone as much as I do him right now.

They lead me through the familiar corridors toward the main entrance and I have to endure gasps from other departments, curious glances and shocked expressions as we appear to do a tour of Media Corp to highlight my shame.

I've been fired, publicly humiliated and without any chance to explain myself. I'm finished.

Finally, we make it outside and I blink in the unexpected sunlight that greets me from the dark place in my mind.

I briefly register the black SUV with blackened windows waiting by the entrance and don't have time to catch my breath as they bundle me inside. The two security guards squeeze in beside me and my last view of the man who made this all happen is his dark penetrating gaze as he slams the door shut and hits the roof with a resounding thud.

Before I can catch my breath, the car speeds away, taking me to God only knows where—well, God and the destructive, domineering, dangerous Dexter Prince.

CHAPTER 5

DEXTER

Strangely, I watch the car disappear from view with an interest that surprises me.

Sir.

The word won't leave me as I roll it around my mind and savor the feeling it gives me. Just the sound of it falling from her lips made me hard and my first look at the woman herself caught my interest despite the anger I'm feeling toward her right now.

Long dark hair that looks as wild as the look in her eyes as she suffered the ultimate humiliation. The way she walked toward me on those impossibly high heels almost made me smile as I sense her need to wear them due to the fact she's shorter than average.

My attention was immediately grabbed by the biggest tits I've ever seen dancing before my eyes like every man's dream. Yes, Holly Bryant was a nice surprise for my eyes, but a kick in the balls for my ego.

She's dangerous. I must remember that because she has cast doubt on my loyalty and almost got me killed. I'm angry, vengeful and liable to do her some serious damage the way I'm feeling now and so, for her own safety, I removed her from my side almost immediately.

Sir. Interesting how that made me feel. Maybe I should re-think this whole situation because it could make what's about to happen all the more enjoyable—for me.

I head back to my office and wonder what's she's thinking now. No doubt confused, fearful, and probably angry. She looked feisty, a woman who takes no shit and I like those qualities in a woman. Maybe I will enjoy tearing the truth from her because Holly Bryant may have been fired from Media Corp, but she's about to discover she hasn't got away lightly. Her nightmare is only just beginning and as I have no feeling inside me whatsoever, it's a bumpy road ahead—for her.

The phone rings and Helen says breathlessly, "Mr. King is calling."

"Put him through."

I settle back in my chair as Ryder says abruptly, *"Is it done?"*

"Yes. The woman herself is currently traveling to my ranch where she will be kept for questioning."

"I see." There's a brief silence and then he says abruptly, *"Remember, we don't have long. Find out what she knows and send it through because we need all the time we've got. I could interrogate her myself; it may help speed up the process."*

"I'm sure it would." I laugh softly.

"However, I'm more than interested to discover how she bypassed my system and submitted that article to the press without my authorization. No, leave it with me and if I fail, I'll call and hand the baton to you."

Ryder sounds almost hopeful. *"Then move fast, Dexter because I'm an impatient man and don't forget..."*

He pauses and I swear my heart rate increases.

"We're counting on you."

He cuts the call and as I replace the receiver, I feel a real fear. Not just from him, but for the situation we find ourselves in. Five Kings all with a role to play in keeping society moving in the right direction. Every single one of us bar one has been tested, challenged and threatened and we are not in the clear yet. Someone wants to bring us down, and it's becoming increasingly obvious they will succeed because if Ryder's right and this thing comes to a head in two weeks, the sands of time are about to explode and cover the world in shit.

Somehow, I manage to get through the day and set in place my absence from the office. Meetings are arranged, instructions given and jobs allocated, freeing me from my daily business to concentrate on a far more important one. Saving the Five Kings. Saving me.

7 pm and Helen has left already because I sent her home with instructions to keep me updated. All my staff need to know is that I'm taking a vacation and may be away for three weeks to a month. I will work from home and expect updates in the usual way.

Physically, I will be removed from my business, but mentally I am still running things, which says a lot for modern technology because I intend on playing with my prey for as long as it takes.

Making my way to the rooftop of the building I rule with a rod of iron, I see the chopper waiting. David, my pilot, nods as I approach and my bodyguard holds open the door. "Thanks, Sam."

I nod as he says respectfully, "Evening, Dexter, everything has been arranged as per your instructions."

"Good."

As I settle in my seat and reach for my phone, I feel a sense of satisfaction that one area of my life appears to be running smoothly at least. Yes, it's the part that's out of control that needs addressing, and Holly Bryant holds the key to that information.

The chopper takes off with my pilot and bodyguard sitting in the front and I turn my attention to business as we fly toward my ranch set in the middle of nowhere, where nobody will hear her screams.

CHAPTER 6

HOLLY

*N*ow I'm fucking terrified. There is zero conversation, and it's pretty obvious when we reach the town border that they're not taking me home.

"What's going on?" Even my voice sounds weak and afraid and I hate the person I've morphed into right now and yet all I'm greeted with is a wall of silence.

I can't even fight, struggle, or escape because the mountain of steel I'm sitting between is an impenetrable barrier of muscle formed around men who obviously don't have the ability to string a sentence together.

If I close my eyes and open them again, I'm hoping this is just a nightmare because what the hell is happening to me?

My voice shakes as I say, "Please, where are we going?"

Again, they just stare straight ahead and I know there will be no polite conversation happening with these two stone menaces.

The tinted windows prevent anyone looking in and my heart lurches when I see a set of handcuffs in the inside pocket of one of the guards.

I watch in disbelief as the familiar landscape changes to a barren one and the road appears to stretch endlessly in front of me. The only thing that happens on the journey is the bottle of water placed in my hands by one of the silent guards.

The car is fast and the silence oppressive, and I wonder if they are taking me to an early grave. The landscape is devoid of plants or vegetation, telling me we're heading into the scrub desert and my heart thumps frantically inside me as I try to make sense of what's going on.

I feel so tired, sore and desperate to stretch as the minutes turn to hours and nothing changes. Despite the comfort of the car and the air conditioning that keeps an even temperature, I find myself in the scariest situation of my life and try desperately to plan my escape from it.

Desperately hoping we must stop for fuel, the restroom, or food, I decide to plead a call of nature and somehow escape from them. Maybe there will be someone who could help me, alert the authorities, anything. I don't even have my purse because it's right where I left it at Media Corp. I have nothing but my tortured thoughts as I sense my life is over almost as soon as it began, after one moment of insanity.

Why did I take that chance? I am the biggest fool because there's a reason Dexter Prince is the king of media. He's ruthless and yet I never really expected I'd register on his radar - ever. Why is a small story so damaging? Why is he so angry, it doesn't make sense?

Thinking of the source of my story, I wonder if he knew it would provoke this reaction. It makes me fear for him and I wonder if he knows this is happening. Perhaps he can alert the authorities, but then again, how would he know? Nothing in my life makes sense anymore and as my life flashes before my eyes, I try to make sense of the situation I have fallen into.

I'm not even sure how long, or how far we travel because by

the time the car grinds to a halt, I appear to have fallen asleep and wake with a start.

Before I can register where we are, I am pulled roughly from the car and given no time to plan a misguided escape. Is this it, am I to expect a bullet in the head and an open grave to fall into? It certainly feels that way, and yet as the security light illuminates the path, I notice we have arrived at some kind of building.

The two guards take an arm each and almost drag me toward a door set in a stone wall and I do the only thing I can and scream so loudly it almost shatters my own eardrums. "Shut the fuck up, there's nobody around to hear you, anyway."

The first words the man on my right speaks sound angry, rough and unforgiving and as the tears stream down my face, I am pushed roughly through the door and it slams behind me.

I stumble and reach out and, finding nothing, fall to a heap on the ground that is hard against my knees. It hurts like hell and I gasp as pain shoots through me as my knee scrapes against what appears to be concrete.

As my eyes adjust to the darkness, I see the faint outlines of a metal bed and chair in the corner of the room. There are no windows and I shiver as I imagine anything could be in here right now and I feel my heart thumping out of control. I'm a prisoner. It's obvious. This room has no luxuries, no mod cons and is designed to strike fear in its occupant's heart. I can't see a thing and just sit shivering on the cold ground wondering what the hell just happened.

Suddenly, a light flickers and illuminates the room in a dim glow, and I look around in disbelief. I was right, this is a prison and the single metal bed with nothing but a thin gray blanket mocks me as I crawl toward it. The stone walls are cold and filled with cobwebs and the chair is placed above a bucket that can only mean one thing. This is it. Complete humiliation because this appears to be my new home for as long as that bastard says it is.

What the fuck did I do to deserve this? I wrote a story, big deal, I'm a reporter, it's what we do. The man's mad, insane, a lunatic and I'm now at his mercy.

Looking around, I can't see anything I can use to defend myself against the monster and as my situation hits home, I start to shake—with rage.

How dare he? I could kill him with my bare hands. The man's deranged, villainous and so screwed when I make it out of here and report him to the cops. Dexter Prince had better not show his face again because I'm likely to alter it permanently and if I have to be in prison, I may as well go down for his murder because at least then it would be deserved.

What sort of fucking madman fires someone, then kidnaps and tosses them in a prison that I wouldn't keep a dog in?

I am actually fuming and quite honestly, I'm glad of my anger to keep me warm because this place is freezing. There must be some kind of air conditioning in here because there's a heatwave outside, which is why I'm wearing totally unsuitable clothes for arctic temperatures.

I'm hungry, tired, freezing and afraid. My defenses are down, and I'm trying to deal with every emotion under the sun right now.

Grabbing the thin gray blanket, I wrap it around myself and start pacing. I know better than to waste my energy screaming. I'm not stupid and know these thick walls are impenetrable in every way. There is nobody around to hear my screams, that's a bit obvious right now and I have no answers to any of the questions that are burning inside me right now.

I don't even want to touch that disgusting bed and it took all my human survival skills just to touch the grimy old blanket. The only weapon I have is these impossibly high heels and so as soon as that door opens, I intend on being behind it ready to attack. Now I'm angry and liable to piss in the bucket and throw the contents at the first person through that door because God help me if I'm about to end my days here, I'm not going down without a fight.

CHAPTER 7

DEXTER

*W*e circle the ranch and I feel the excitement intensify. I'm home.

I love my ranch. I come here so rarely I still feel the thrill when we touch down on the landing pad and my ranch hand meets me in the jeep.

Jason is waiting with a smile on his leather-tanned face and his bright blue eyes twinkle under his cowboy hat as he says respectfully, "Good to see you, Dexter."

"You too, Jason, everything good?"

"Sure is, as always. Nothing to report except Jolene's expecting to calf in the early hours, so I'm in for an all-nighter."

"Need a hand?"

"Only if you insist." He grins and I smile with a happiness I only appear to feel here. Out here, there are no responsibilities. I have total freedom to live a basic life with no deadlines, no meetings and just nature to calm my spirit. I wonder what Jason thinks of my visitor and say with interest, "And my visitor?"

"Safely in her room."

He looks as if he has a thousand questions, but wisely keeps them to himself as he smiles. "Maisy's got your food ready. You must be hungry."

"Can't wait."

I step into the jeep beside him and Sam jumps in the back and we set off over the rough ground toward the main house.

Maisy and Jason look after my ranch in return for bed, board and a home. I don't count them as employees though, more like friends, possibly even family because aside from Helen and anyone who I meet through business, they are the only people I talk to other than Sam.

I have distanced myself from society, including my family, because of the biggest mistake of my life and the only visitors I ever entertain are the whores back at my penthouse in the city. Not here, though. I bring nobody here - until her.

Maisy beams as I walk through the door. "Good to see you, Dexter. I made your favorite, beef ribs and fries."

I can smell the mouth-watering dish waiting for me and instantly relax. "You're an angel."

She laughs softly and hands me a beer that's so cold it instantly freezes my fingers.

"So, Jason tells me you're staying a while, and your visitor?"

She looks curious, and I shrug. "Business, Maisy, unpleasant business that hopefully won't take long."

"I see." I can tell she disapproves from the tightness to her jaw and who can blame her. Imprisoning a young girl in the cow barn isn't really that hospitable, and I know they will be uncomfortable with that. They trust me though, which is a good thing because I barely trust myself these days. There's an anger inside me that is gaining momentum instead of dulling with time. My release from it is being an irritable bastard and boxing, but I am fast realizing that I'm only able to control it through dominant sex. Whores are good at playing the submissive, but it's not enough.

Once again, my thoughts turn to Holly and I feel something

stirring inside me that hasn't been there for some time. Can I do this? Can I use her to drive away my demons?

Sir. One word that sealed her fate along with that brave set to her jaw as she walked toward me, looking like every fucking depraved thought in my mind. I could ruin that girl and not even break a sweat and extract the information I need in the cruelest of ways. The idea just won't go away and fills me with an excitement I haven't had for some time.

The ball is now firmly in her court because she will only get out of this mess if she gives me what I want. Information and how I get that information will be all the better for me if she takes her time. Yes, two weeks will be more than enough to ruin Holly Bryant and purge my demons a little more.

Thinking of her cold and shivering in the cow barn makes me hard already. I need to break this woman and find out what she knows and like every general, it will be done on the back of hard decisions and no mercy.

So, I eat my food, relish the fact I'm home and then watch the game in my living room with a cold beer to keep me company. Then I take a long, cold shower and run through just what I'm going to do to Holly Bryant when I get my hands on her.

I'm up early and the sound of the rooster's call makes me smile. There is no sound other than nature and the gentle breeze that wafts through the open window. The large comfortable bed wraps me in comfort, and I feel the stress fall away as I contemplate the day ahead.

Dressing in black jeans and a tight tee, I head down to breakfast and my mouth waters when I smell the freshly cooked pancakes and bacon sizzling on the skillet. Maisy and Jason are already in the large kitchen and Sam is watching the morning news bulletin as I pull up a chair and reach for the coffee.

"Anything of interest?"

I cock a brow toward the television and he smiles. "Nothing out of the ordinary. Just as we planned."

Thinking of what could have been breaking news right now, I thank God that Ryder intercepted the article. But how? How did my system not pick it up and why was it approved on auto?

Sam lifts his mug and says thoughtfully. "Any idea how it slipped through the net?"

"I'm hoping our visitor can explain that."

He nods. "Do you think she's a spy?"

"Possibly, but who for?"

"A rival mogul perhaps, someone out to seize your crown."

"I doubt it. I think this goes way past that."

"In what way?" Sam looks interested, and I shrug. "Personal stuff."

He nods and knows better than to question me because the Five Kings is an organization only I know about. It's safer that way and the less anybody outside the organization knows, the better, which is why Holly's article is so toxic because there was information in there that could only have come from the inside out.

My good mood vanishes when I think about what's at stake and I think long and hard through breakfast about how I'm going to approach this.

By the time we've finished and Sam heads off to do what I pay him for, I am left to contemplate the day ahead.

Maisy clears away and I say quickly, "Has she eaten yet?"

"I was waiting for you; shall I take her a tray?"

"I'll do it."

She nods and I know she can't wait to catch a look at the woman I've got under lock and key, but it's best to keep Holly away from the homestead and extract my information in a closed environment.

As I take the tray and begin the walk, I wonder what I'll find. She's sure to be pissed and will probably try to fight her way out. The thought amuses me and I almost hope she does.

That's why I'm surprised when I open the door and head inside, to find her sitting on the chair facing me, with her hands in her lap, looking as if she's about to attend an interview.

She fixes me with a steady gaze and none of the fear I expected to find. The room has a musty smell and I notice the bed has been tidied and the woman herself appears composed and unemotional.

For a moment we just stare at one another and I look for any flicker of fear and feel annoyed there is only a slight spark of derision in her eyes. She looks as if I'm a pile of shit that blew in and, for some reason, that excites me more than her fear.

"Holly."

I set the tray down on the bed and say abruptly, "Your breakfast, I'm guessing you must be hungry."

Just the slight tremble to her bottom lip reveals how many emotions she's hiding right now, and she nods.

"Thank you."

I'm curious because she's acting as if this is a normal daily event and it throws me a little, so I say blankly, "Any questions?"

"It appears that you are the one with questions, Mr. Prince, otherwise I wouldn't be here."

"Good answer."

"Was it a test, forgive me, I would have studied for it if I'd known?"

I lean against the back of the door and fix her with a dead look.

"Aren't you curious, you're a reporter, it should be second nature to ask questions?"

"I figured you'd get around to telling me why you fired me for doing my job in a callous, brutal way and then kidnapped me and imprisoned me in a shit palace."

Her eyes flash and I smile to myself. This is interesting.

"The article you submitted without authorization. I need to know where you got your information."

I come right out with it and hope to hell she doesn't give me what I want right away because this woman is surprising me and I want to be the one to break that calm exterior and hear her scream.

"Mr. Prince." Her tone is measured, almost pleasant as she says firmly, "The first rule of journalism is you never reveal your source. I shouldn't need to tell you that and you should also know that it doesn't matter how I came across the story, it's the content that counts. Was it a lie, are you telling me my information was wrong in some way?"

She's too cool, too self-assured and I don't like it—one bit. If anything, she should be begging me and pleading for her release. Not making me feel like I'm some kind of novice at this.

"I don't care what the rules are, I make them up as I go along, anyway. You were under my employ and as your boss, I want to know where you got your information. There's nothing wrong with that, so tell me."

"No."

Her reply is curt and edged in steel, and I love the way her eyes flash as she faces me down.

Sighing, I reach out and lift the tray and remove the glass of water from it, setting it down on the floor.

"Then I'll bid you good day, Miss. Bryant. Let me know when you're ready to talk and I'll give you food. I'll return in two hours; I trust you'll rethink your foolish decision because the sooner you give me what I want, the sooner you can go."

I back out of the room and she says quickly, "Wait, you'll let me go if I tell you."

Feeling almost disappointed it was this easy, I nod. "Of course."

She shakes her head and snarls, "And if I don't?"

"Then welcome to your new home. I hope you'll be happy here."

"You can't keep me here, it's against the law."

"Possibly, but I've already explained I don't play by the same rules and I've done my homework and nobody will miss you, anyway."

It's as if I've slapped her in the face because she blanches and I feel a momentary flash of pleasure. The first blow has landed and I revel in her pain.

Slamming the door behind her, I head back to the ranch. Two hours should loosen her tongue a little, and if I'm sure of anything, it's that.

CHAPTER 8

HOLLY

I can't believe what just happened. Dexter Prince stood in that doorway and admitted I was a prisoner. He wants my informant's name and yet how can I betray him? He's family. It's never going to happen because if I've learned one thing, he's a sadistic bastard who gets off on this. The low blow about nobody missing me hit me hard.

He's right. I have no one. My stepbrother has become an email and I can't even remember what he looks like. He could pass me in the street and I'd walk on by. My father is so wrapped up in business he doesn't surface for months on end and the last time I heard from him was two years ago before his tour of the Middle East. The only reason I know he's alive is because his wife forwards me the part in his letters that asks how I am.

Thinking about his wife Amelia, my heart hardens. A woman with no regard for anyone other than her so-called friends and endless social life. She never had any time for her new husband's daughter and had me bundled off to school for months on end, so she didn't have to bother with me. Her son suffered the same treatment, which is why he's so weird, probably.

Colton Jeffrey is the kind of guy you expect to see on America's Most Wanted one day. Seriously creepy and totally weird, which is why it was such a shock when he offered to help with my career.

Thinking about him, I wonder why I feel the need to protect him like this. I should toss his name out there and gain my freedom, because he's probably involved in serious shit, anyway.

But something about the way Dexter Prince demands answers by force riles me up. It's no longer about the answers he needs, it's him. I don't want to break and give him what he wants because I'm a stubborn woman who likes a fight.

When he stood before me, I hated that my mouth watered at the sight of him. How can someone so fucked up be so attractive? It's not fair, but just the sight of those strong arms holding the tray and the wicked glint in his eyes, made me want to please him. There was something so intoxicating about the gentle act of bringing me food himself and the dominant edge that made me wet. It interested me way more than it should because he's like fire and ice all rolled into a sexy package of insanity.

I never thought I'd be that woman who craved a man caressing her cheek while staring deep into her eyes before demanding she takes her panties off. I'm almost disappointed he didn't. In fact, he couldn't look any more disinterested if he tried, which hurt. He thinks he's better than me. Above me, that I'm worthless, an irritant that needs to be dealt with before lunch.

My stomach growls, reminding what a fucking idiot I am because that food made my mouth water almost as much as the man serving it.

Maybe I should lower my guard, eat the food, tell the man

what he wants to know and go job hunting. At least I'd be free. I don't owe Colton shit, but something is holding me back.

I'm left with my own thoughts churning in my head for the two hours he promised and this time when the door opens, I'm lying back on the bed staring at the ceiling as if the answer lies there.

For a moment he just stares and a shiver runs through me as his gaze lingers on my body, mainly my breasts, just a little longer than necessary and my own darts to the bulge in his pants that surely can't be normal. I'm mildly curious to see for myself if it's as big as it looks and as I tear my gaze upward, I'm met with a smirk and feel my cheeks burn.

"Are you ready to talk?"

"Are you ready to stop acting like a dumbass?"

He raises his eyes. "You really called me a dumbass."

I nod, eyeing the tray hungrily. "If the description fits, live with it."

Moving into an upright position, I stare at the tray that now holds a club sandwich with some potato chips and a large glass of juice and my mouth actually waters as he advances slowly. "So, the name I need, what is it?"

Raising my eyes, I stare into the pit of hell as I say sweetly, "It's, go fuck yourself."

He nods and steps back and then I watch the nice guy disappear as he slams the tray against the wall and the contents smash to the ground. The juice pools on the floor and the chips scatter as the sandwich smashes into the liquid. I could cry when I see the food I so badly need right now disintegrate before my eyes and Dexter advances and pulls me up and toward him with a roughness that strangely excites me. My mouth is dangerously close to his as he snarls, "Then eat your food from the floor like a dog because I'm done with playing nice. Tell me what I want to know or suffer even more humiliation. I've got the rest of my life. What about you?"

He pushes me back and storms from the room and as the door slams, I feel the tears build as the shock sets in. I've prodded the beast and he bites. Why am I so stupid and when will I ever learn?

HE DOESN'T COME BACK. The hours roll past and the time drags interminably. I pace my cell and I'm ashamed to admit I eat what has survived from the floor. The only liquid I have is the bottle of water that he left earlier.

Left alone with my thoughts, I've decided I'm shit company. I'm going stir crazy and it's not even twenty-four hours yet.

After what feels like days but is probably just several hours, the door opens and a man appears that catches me off-guard.

He isn't surprised to see me and just looks me up and down, which instantly gets my back up and I feel fearful for what he may do.

Surely Dexter hasn't sent him in to torture me, or worse. I wouldn't put it past him and now I am immediately regretting being so stubborn.

"Miss. Bryant, please follow me."

He nods respectfully and I stare at him in shock.

"What's going on?"

"Just follow me." He is cool and unemotional and I should really prefer this guy to Dexter, who scares the hell out of me but somehow excites me way more. My head is so scrambled right now because I wasn't expecting this, but then my survival instinct kicks in and I sense my chance to escape. The door is open and freedom beckons—or death. It's fifty-fifty right now and so I take a deep breath and head toward whichever one it is.

As I reach the door, he says darkly, "I should just explain there is nowhere to run, so don't get any ideas. Mr. Prince has decided you will be more comfortable in the main house."

I blink in astonishment. "He did?"

The man nods curtly.

"So, unless you want to remain here, it's best to just follow me and accept your situation."

I nod, but my mind is crowded with possibility right now. This is good, more than good. I could plan my escape from the house. There must be a phone, possibly someone to get on my side. I could be free if I just play my cards close to my chest.

As I follow the man from my dungeon, I take deep breaths of fresh air. It feels good to be outside. The walls were stifling and the air rank inside that hell hole.

As we walk, I notice a pretty pathway lined by flowers and shrubs, and it has a really pleasant vibe. "Where are we?"

I risk a question but am met with a stony silence. Rude.

Sizing up my escort, I quickly come to the conclusion I would lose in a fight and so I try to be clever about this because my first instinct is to slam him in the head with my killer heel and run for the forest that sits in the distance. However, from the look of the man, he races in the Olympics for fun and could snap my neck without breaking a sweat, so I follow him meekly and try to formulate a plan instead.

One thing's for sure, I'm excited. This is unexpected. A glimmer of hope in the darkness. I'm being taken to the main house where anything could happen.

CHAPTER 9

DEXTER

*O*nce I calmed down, I decided to alter my approach. It's obvious keeping her locked in a cell isn't working and part of me admires her strength. However, we don't have time for this and I need that name and fast, so I decided a softer approach may work better. A charm offensive. Get her on side and encourage her to open up and trust me.

Sam persuaded me that I was playing this all wrong and I suppose he has a point. I just never thought she would be so determined. I have to admire her for it because she's right. A journalist never reveals their source, but she should also know that when your boss asks, you jump as high as he tells you to.

Now it's time to extract the information I need in a much more hospitable way, which will make Maisy and Jason happy at least. I know they disapprove of my methods but are too loyal to call me out on them and so I instructed Maisy to make up the guest room and the rest of my staff to act as lookouts to make sure Holly doesn't try to escape. Not that she would get very far, but just in case, the keys to all vehicles have been locked in the safe and the phones disconnected. There is no possible way for her to gain her freedom and so, aside from my own personal office, the rest of the house is now in lockdown. As the key to my office is firmly in my pocket, she won't have a chance in hell of getting anywhere near it.

Tonight, I have instructed Maisy to make us a meal designed to relax my guest and make her feel more comfortable. She must be starving and could really do with something to take the edge off the raging appetite she must have. The table has been set for two and as I make my way to the dining room, I wonder how she'll be. Angry, undoubtedly, but I'm hoping that anger can be channeled the right way because I have decided to seduce my guest and then once I have what I need, send her packing.

As I sit and wait, I swirl the whiskey in a fine arc in the crystal glass and feel strangely excited. This is different, so different. I have never held anyone by force before and it's turning me on so badly. Either that or the thought of the person I'm holding because Holly Bryant is my type to the letter. If I had drawn a picture of my perfect woman, it's her and just imagining holding such a woman makes this a much more interesting project.

My usual whores are dark and sultry and do exactly what I require of them. Occasionally I date and take a woman to bed afterward, however that is unusual because I can't stand the drama that follows. However, drama can be exciting when you're the one writing the script and as I contemplate what I'm going to do with this woman, I feel an excitement that I haven't felt for some time.

I hear her coming before Sam pushes her into the room because her killer heels click on the flagstones.

I look up as she enters and Sam catches my eye and nods. "Miss. Bryant, sir."

He steps back and I know will take up his position outside the room just in case she decides to make a run for it and as the door closes, I consider my guest.

She stands there looking at me with defiance flashing from those beautiful brown eyes. She has obviously showered and the clothes that Maisy laid out for her cling to her curves like a second skin. A black silk dress that ripples as she moves and outlines those impossibly large breasts like a silken glove holding them in place. Her newly washed hair gleams and her eyes flash as she stares at me with such a look of hatred it makes my cock harden almost immediately.

"Miss. Bryant, I trust your new arrangement is to your liking."

She shrugs and leans against the door and stares at me like I'm a bad smell.

"I would rather my own home. So, what's this, have you decided to try to charm the information from me now, classic?"

Resisting the urge to laugh, I pour her a glass of champagne and head across.

"No, I just decided that incarcerating a woman didn't sit well with me and thought I'd offer my hospitality instead. You see, Holly, I'm not an ogre, I do have a heart."

"That's a matter of opinion."

She waves away the glass of champagne and says shortly, "Water will be fine. I don't drink and certainly not on an empty stomach."

Setting the glass down, I nod. "Noted. Then please, take your seat and allow me to remedy that immediately."

She moves to the end of the table where a place has been set and, as I hold out her chair, she laughs. "Cut the crap, Mr. Prince, you're no gentleman. I can see through your act and I'm not biting. Just tell me you've called me a cab and I'll be happy."

Suddenly, Ryder's offer of interrogation is looking very appealing right now because how the fuck does anyone get information when the person is as stubborn as she is?

Luckily, Maisy enters and I note her curious glance at Holly as she sets the food on the table and Holly looks surprised to see her.

Maisy smiles sweetly and as Holly opens her mouth to speak, I say quickly, "That will be all Maisy."

She nods and leaves before Holly can speak and as the door closes, she says with some surprise, "Who was that?"

"My housekeeper."

"That figures."

"What does?"

"Even your housekeeper looks like a Playboy Bunny. You know you are so stereotypical it's not even funny, sad really."

Taking my seat at the opposite end of the table, I laugh softly. "Then I'll enjoy proving you wrong about me."

Raising my glass to her in a salute, I say, "Here's to a new friendship."

She just shakes her head and pointedly ignores me.

I watch as she eyes up the food and know her stomach must be desperate to get started, so I say quickly, "Anyway, we may as well eat and you can tell me more about how you came to work for me."

She almost falls on the food and as I watch her eat, a thousand images of what I'd prefer her to do with that sexy mouth entertains me.

Maisy has excelled herself and the basic meal of meat, potatoes, and green veg melts in the mouth and the fine wine that accompanies it makes me relax a little as I watch my guest like a tiger stalking its prey.

The lamplight illuminates her flushed face as she devours the meal with a hunger that's not unexpected but a delight to watch. She obviously appreciates good food, despite the fact she's hungry and would probably eat a rabid rat right now.

She drinks the entire jug of water in no time at all and I feel ashamed at how I've treated her so far. It's not me, the heartless brute who doesn't consider a woman's feelings. I prefer a softer approach, where she would most likely end up in my bed.

Feeling glad I changed direction, I say with interest, "So, Holly Bryant, would be journalist and guardian of information, tell me about yourself."

"What do you want to know, apart from my informant's name of course?"

Now she's eaten, she's relaxed a little and her soft laugh takes me by surprise. It completely lights up her face and the red glow to her cheeks enhances her beauty and, quite honestly, takes my breath away.

"Well, I'd like to know what made you apply for a position in my company."

"What's this an interview? I already had one of those and guess what, I got the job."

She raises her glass of water to me in a mock salute, and I shake my head. "Typical journalist, can't answer a fucking question to save your life."

She looks at me and a broad smile breaks out across her face and she laughs. It surprises me a little as it totally transforms her. The sullen, guarded woman has changed into one who is vibrant, exciting and full of fun and it takes all my strength not to openly stare.

"Well, Mr. Prince, for your information, I have wanted to work for you since I graduated High School. Reporting fascinates me and the more I studied it, the more I wanted it. So, I set my goals and only wanted the best."

"I take it that meant me." I laugh to blur the cocky statement, and she grins. "Of course, why settle for less than the best. I owe it to myself to strive for perfection, although the rag you call the Globe is far from that, but we've all got to start somewhere."

"What's wrong with it?"

"What's right with it. Gutter journalism chasing sensationalism."

"You're wrong, Holly, it's a publication that highlights the failings of the human who gets it wrong most of the time. Greed, desire and ambition overshadow what is right. It's the ten commandments on speed because there is nothing more interesting than watching people in the public eye getting it wrong on every level. It makes the rest of us feel good about our own choices in life and makes us pity those who outwardly appear to have done well for themselves. Sensationalism sells and we reap the rewards of that, so before you dismiss my business so cruelly, know the facts first and learn from them."

She stares at me in surprise and, for the first time, she looks at me a little differently. There's an expression of admiration on her face that strokes my already inflated ego and a reverence that I wouldn't mind seeing on her face as she kneels before me naked and ready to suck my cock.

It appears the game has changed and now the players are in place, it's time to begin.

CHAPTER 10

HOLLY

*M*y head is scrambled one hundred percent. The man I thought I hated has surprised me again—this time in a good way.

When I stepped into the room, I almost melted because he is something else. Dashing good looks outlined in darkness. The air that surrounds him is intense and toxic and just seeing those dark eyes staring at me as if he can't wait to rip the clothes off my back and make me do insane things to him, had me squirming inside because I absolutely hate the attraction I have toward Dexter fucking Prince.

I shouldn't be interested in a maniac, but I am. I shouldn't desire him as much as I do, but my body had other ideas. I shouldn't inwardly pant at the sight of the power that flashes from his eyes and imagine that mouth bringing me so much pleasure it would ruin me forever—it does. I should guard against this man because he could ruin me in a far more destructive way than just locking me in a cold prison with no food.

Now my situation has changed because I have something I always desired. Him. A one on one with the great man himself and although the circumstances are a little fucked up, now's my chance to learn from the master. This is pure gold and I need to play this to my advantage because, despite my hatred for the man, my admiration beats it down every time. He's my idol, the man I had a picture of on my dorm wall to remind me to strive to be excellent. He doesn't need to know that though and so I keep my girlish infatuation in check and stare at him with a guarded look.

"So, tell me how you started, Mr. Prince."

He actually laughs. "Call me Dexter and don't think I haven't noticed you have turned the tables on me, Holly. Maybe I should re-think your position in my company."

"I don't have one. You publicly fired me, humiliated me and then kidnapped and starved me. You're not really selling this job to be honest and we haven't even discussed my salary."

"Maybe we can negotiate, that could be fun."

My mouth dries as he directs that wicked look my way and an image of me sweeping the plates aside and demanding he take me right now is quickly pushed away. The sexual tension between us is off the scale and suddenly the game changes in a nano-second as he undresses me with those dark, deadly eyes.

It's difficult to tear my own away from his and every reason why I should is screaming inside my head. *'He's playing you, he's not interested, he wants information, you're nothing to him. Don't do it, Holly.'*

Then there's that weak bitch who wins every time, shouting, *'You want this, get your man, this is a once in a lifetime chance, don't sweat it, just run with it and fuck the bastard.'*

"Holly."

His deep voice brings my attention back to him and the knowing smirk on his face tells me he can read minds as well and feeling a little flustered I say slightly breathlessly, "I don't suppose you have any more water."

He pushes his own jug toward me and I fall on it like the Ancient Mariner.

"So, you don't drink, that's admirable."

"Not really. I don't drink champagne and definitely no alcohol on an empty stomach. I prefer red wine actually, full bodied and deep."

I almost groan at that bitch who is openly flirting with him because she has apparently woken up and taken charge of my senses and the interest in his eyes is causing strange things to happen to me inside.

My heart almost gives out on me as he stands and lifts a bottle of wine from the table and heads my way. He doesn't speak, just stares, and that is the most unnerving thing of all. I watch as he splashes some of the liquid into a wine glass and without even tasting it, I know it will be the finest wine I have ever tasted because this man expects the best and demands it as standard.

Setting the bottle down next to me, he says huskily, "This is yours. Now you've eaten, you may as well indulge your passion a little, that's the fun part."

He heads back to his seat while I squirm on mine because this man should be called Sexter Prince because every word, every gesture, is like a sexual act and I'm fast realizing I'm way out of my depth here and struggling to remain afloat.

Grabbing the glass, I savor the feeling of the liquid coating me inside and caressing my body in decadence. Even the wine is stripping my resistance and as the man himself watches me from across the table, I have an overwhelming urge to give him whatever he wants, and I mean, anything.

"So, Holly, tell me your ambitions. I'm guessing they are still intact despite this latest setback."

Clearing my throat, I pull my mind from the gutter and switch to my professional one.

"I have big ambitions, Mr. Pr…"

"Dexter, I will only tell you that one more time."

He appears angry and I nod "Dexter, yes, um, well…" Just saying his name feels like a violation and I take another sip of wine and pray for a fast shot of courage to get me through this meal.

"Well, until I hit a speed bump in my road to success, my plan was to work my ass off, learn the business and then one day take what I learned and start my own publication."

As I say the words, I realize how juvenile they sound because I am talking to the man who runs the whole media circus in the country. To his credit, he doesn't laugh and just humors me with a nod. "Impressive ambition, I wish you well."

"Any tips?" I feel bold enough to ask and he shrugs. "I always find honesty is the best policy."

"In what way?" If I could record this conversation, I would, because any tips from the master are worth more than gold and he sighs. "Just stay true to your principles. Never publish anything that could cause destruction because you may never recover from the effects of it and always check and double check your facts."

For some reason, he looks as if this is a lesson he learned first-hand which makes me curious.

He leans on the table and fixes me with a direct look. "Holly, if I can tell you one thing, it's this. Think about what you write —carefully. You may have the facts, but they are not always truthful. Think about the repercussions of your article and assess if it makes the world a better place, or just serves to destroy rather than inform."

"But doesn't that go against what we do?"

I feel a little confused, and he smiles briefly. "In what way?"

"Well, um, surely it's our job to report the facts and not dress them up to spare feelings. Isn't it the sensationalism that sells your news, makes you money and keeps the customer coming back for more?"

"Of course, but it's knowing what's morally right and wrong that counts. If you publish a story that causes death, would you do it?"

"Of course not." I feel shocked and shake my head vigorously. He sits back in his seat and says darkly. "I speak from experience, Holly. I made a mistake, a costly one, and went ahead with it, anyway. The results of that are something I have to live with for the rest of my life and I wouldn't recommend it. Don't make my mistakes and if I offer you any advice at all, it's that. Which brings me back to the reason you're here."

"I won't…" He holds up his hand.

"I get that. I don't like it, but I understand your code of ethics and admire you for it."

Well, this is a first, and it takes me back a little. "You mean you won't ask me to reveal my source."

He nods. "You know what I want, it's up to you to decide. Let me just say that the information I seek is important. It could have life-changing consequences, which is why I have gone to such lengths to get it. Once again, you don't know all the facts and I'm asking you to trust me with this. It's more important than both of us, Media Corp and has far-reaching repercussions if I don't discover who gave you the information."

For a moment I think he must be kidding me because what the hell?

"Is this a joke?"

"Do I look as if I'm laughing, Holly?" He shifts and fixes me with a dark look. "Think about it. You wrote a story about a powerful man who has great responsibility and trusted the facts you were fed. I'm guessing you know that person enough to believe every word you wrote. What if I told you it was fabricated lies because I know the true story first-hand?"

"Um…" I am actually speechless because I hadn't thought of that. Surely Colton never made this up, for what reason?

Dexter appears to be going in for the kill because he says roughly, "It's not just the story either, it's the fact your article escaped the process and ended up in line to be published. Automatically approved, which concerns me the most. How has my system failed and how have you acquired classified information?"

"I'm sorry." I sound like a child as I realize the enormity of what's happening here and Dexter laughs dully. "For your information, I'm the least of your problems right now. A bigger bastard than me wants to get his hands on you and I'm the only one standing in the way of that."

"What the fuck?"

My eyes are wide with horror and my heart threatening to give out on me as my bleak situation hits me square it the face.

"So, Holly, tell me what you know because we don't have long and if it helps with your conscience, know that you are preventing something that could spell disaster for this country, if not the world."

CHAPTER 11

DEXTER

I think she's got the message. I'm an evil bastard because I relish the sight of the blood draining from her face and the wild look in her eye. She looks as if she's about to pass out as the enormity of her situation hits her hard. She is struggling and I find that strangely fascinating to watch. Her inward struggle is impressive because even now she just can't bring herself to tell me what I want to know.

I keep the pressure up by staring at her—hard, and the flush to her face tells me she's struggling with everything I just said.

In fact, I don't think I've ever seen such a beautiful sight and wish I could take a photo and hang it on the wall to mark the occasion when this woman is faced with the hardest decision of her life—so far.

I decide to heap even more pressure on her and lean forward.

"I have a proposition for you."

"You do."

She licks her lips nervously and sits straight-backed in her chair.

"I believe you are looking for a job right now and I may just have one that would interest you."

"You do?" I love that she is struggling for words because I want to break Holly Bryant and mold her into my fantasy.

"Yes, I would like to mentor you and help your career by taking you on as my assistant. Help you learn as a sort of apprentice. Take you through every department in my organization and at the end of it, when you have proved to me that you have learned every lesson needed to survive, I will set you up with the publication of your choice."

As carrots go, this one is impossible to refuse and I see the emotion in her eyes as she almost crumbles before me.

"Seriously." I think she's going to cry as her lip quivers and she looks one hot mess as she struggles with whatever demons are clawing her back.

"So, one-time offer, Holly. Tell me your source and I give you the world. That is how valuable your information is. Nobody would know but us. What do you say?"

The air is tense and I think I'm even sweating as I lay it on the line and wait for her decision. Her fingers shake as she lifts the wine to her lips and the defeat in her eyes tells me I've won before she even utters the words I so badly need to hear. "My stepbrother."

The words hang in the air, surrounded by confusion. "Your stepbrother."

I stare at her in surprise and she nods, looking as if she's just sacrificed him to Lucifer.

"Colton Jeffrey. He fed me the information and told me it would elevate my career. He made me swear not to reveal his identity because it would put him in danger."

I say nothing and just leave the room. I can tell she's surprised, but I don't have a moment to waste.

As Sam steps forward, I say urgently, "Guard her, I need to deal with the information."

"She told you; man, that was fast."

"Did you ever doubt me, Sam?"

He laughs as I push past him and head straight to my den. Ryder needs this information so we can locate this Colton Jeffrey and find out just where the trail ends.

The relief is a welcome passenger as I sit behind my desk and remove the phone I only use to call the other Five Kings. Momentarily, I wonder if that's wise because there is still one more king who has yet to earn our trust in this. Sighing, I replace it and head off to the kitchen, where I find Maisy washing up and clearing away the debris of our meal preparations. She looks up in surprise as I say quickly, "Please, may I use your phone?"

"Of course."

She whips it from her back pocket and I smile my thanks. "Just a quick text, sorry to ask."

Turning away, I punch in the name and then tap in Ryder's number. Once sent, I delete the message and history and hand it back. "Thanks, darlin'. Lovely meal by the way, my guest enjoyed it."

"Will you be requiring dessert?"

"Sure, why not."

Now the job's done, I can relax a little. I have the information we needed and now I have the interesting company of a woman I've just chained to my side for the next few years. Was it worth it? Just thinking of the woman waiting for me, makes me almost run to get back to her. Yes, it was worth it because this is just the beginning for Holly Bryant and Dexter Prince and only time will tell where this journey takes us and I'm desperate to get started.

CHAPTER 12

HOLLY

*W*hat just happened? I can't believe he left. Almost as soon as the name left my lips, he was gone. Was it all an act that I fell for like a gullible fool? Have I just endangered Colton's life in one moment of greed because, as bargains go, he offered me one I'd be a fool to refuse, but at what cost?

Alone with my thoughts, I am now having second ones because what if he was lying to get what he wants? I wouldn't put that past him and the tears build when I think about how easily I was played.

Reaching for the wine, I fill my glass because oblivion seems the best place for me now because what the hell have I just agreed to?

It must have only been ten minutes before he returns and I'm relieved to see him, which surprises me more than anything.

It's like a force of nature enters the room because now he's all business, reminding me who the man is and what a fool I was to think I could play him at his own game.

"Dessert's on its way."

He takes his seat and smiles, disarming me once again.

"Thank you."

Two words that mean a lot more than anything else right now and I nod, awash with shame for what I've done.

"Thanks."

I almost can't look at him because I feel so angry at myself. I've let my stepbrother down and sacrificed him for personal gain. How can I live with that?

To my surprise, a warm hand tilts my face upward and I'm shocked to see Dexter crouching before me. Then I'm even more surprised when he pulls me against him and wraps his hand around the back of my head and comforts me like he would a child.

"You did the right thing, Holly, don't ever doubt that. If your stepbrother is innocent, he will be fine too. We need to find him to protect him. You did the right thing."

It's too much. The whole situation is like a pile of bricks burying me one by one. I'm battered, bruised, sore and broken. The whole experience has created so much pressure it's just surprising I haven't buckled already and his kindness undoes me in a way I never saw coming. Then, to my surprise, I break down, sobbing like a baby in his arms as he comforts me by whispered words and light kisses on the top of my head.

I don't even register the door opening and look up in surprise when a sweet voice with a southern drawl says kindly, "Maybe you should eat something, honey, you're exhausted."

I look up and see the pretty woman looking down at me with concern and shaking her head with disapproval as she looks at her boss.

She smiles sympathetically as I sniff, "I'm sorry, it's embarrassing really."

Dexter stands and says almost kindly, "It's fine, cry all you want, you should be proud of yourself, not many women could cope with what I've put you through."

He looks at his housekeeper almost apologetically. "I'll leave you to it, see that she's ok and let me know if she needs anything."

I look at him in surprise. "You're leaving me."

"Yes."

His tone is devoid of emotion, curt even, and he says abruptly, "I have work to do. Enjoy your evening, Holly and grab some sleep because the hard work begins tomorrow. 7 am sharp and that's starting off lightly. Your job starts then."

I just stare in confusion as, without another word, he leaves the room and Maisy sighs as the door closes.

"Don't try to understand that man, Miss. Bryant, he's a closed book that lost its key years ago. Just know he means well, most of the time, anyway."

I watch in a trance as she heaps apple pie on a plate and drowns it in cream and says warmly, "I'll fetch you some coffee and then help you find your room. Dexter's right, you need sleep now and everything will seem better in the morning."

"Then why do I feel as if I just sold my soul to the devil?"

She laughs. "Haven't we all, honey, welcome to the club."

DESPITE EVERYTHING, I sleep well, probably because I'm exhausted. The comfortable bed in the pretty room is just what I needed, and I fell into it after a luxurious shower and clean pajamas. I just assumed the clothes were loaned to me by Maisy and never really thought much about it and it's only when I wake and stretch out feeling a lot better, that I note the familiar fabric.

Sitting up, I look down and blink in disbelief because surely this is just a massive coincidence. I have pajamas just like this.

Jumping up, I head to the closet and open it and then close it again just as quickly before checking it again. Carefully folded and hung in order of color appear to be the contents of my closet from home.

The familiar sight mocks me as I sift through the rails and a cold feeling washes over me. These are my clothes, but how?

Looking through the racks of shoes, opening drawers and trying to take it in, I wonder how the hell the contents of my closet have found their way here?

That's not all. When I head back into the room, I see various personal effects from my apartment dotted around and even my purse sitting pretty on the table underneath the window.

Quickly, I grab hold of it and check for my phone because this is seriously creepy and I haven't got a clue what is happening here.

The phone is missing.

Checking again, it's obvious there is nothing here that can connect me to the outside world. No iPad, no phone. Just everything else.

My make-up, my jewelry and my notebook.

As I stare at the notebook, a cold feeling creeps over me as I open the page with trembling fingers and see the notes I've made on the information Colton sent me. I already know Dexter will have seen this and the anxiety almost knocks me senseless because there is so much more than the story about Hunter Blake. There are pages of details about Dexter too. Private stuff that I feel physically sick thinking he read and confidential information about his family, his past and his private life. If I feel anything right now, it's shame. It's one thing to write a story but if he sees this, it's like a personal assault. How would I feel if I saw pages of details of my own life carefully documented to be used against me?

I feel sick and hate myself more than he must right now because I have pushed aside my principles as I pursued my dream, and the person who made it happen was Colton.

Just thinking about my stepbrother creates a different kind

of feeling inside me. I always knew there was something not quite right about him. The creepy way his eyes would follow me when I left a room. The way he looked at me as if he could read my mind and the uneasy way he had of appearing out of the shadows when I thought I was alone.

Why is he doing this though, it doesn't make sense and as my mind struggles to understand that I have been played for some form of personal gain, I absolutely hate how that makes me feel?

CHAPTER 13

DEXTER

I am so angry I can't think straight. I think I was up most of the night reading the copies I made of Holly's journal. A book of damnation—hers because reading this proves to me I was right not to trust anyone and never let them close. This woman has scripted the pages of her downfall because she knows everything.

My dirty secrets are laid bare before my eyes and it's not for comfortable reading. Not just me either. Personal details on all the five kings have been listed in a journal of devastation and I breathe a sigh of relief that I caught this in time before they made it out into the public domain.

Then again, they already are if Holly has access to them because whoever fed her this shit knew exactly what they were doing.

The conversation I shared with Ryder last night left me in no doubt what was at stake. As soon as her belongings reached me, courtesy of my men raiding her apartment, I sat down to sift through her life. I know it was wrong, but there is no right in this when you are struggling to survive the most destructive storm.

Ryder is now actively looking for her stepbrother and I almost pity him, but when you play with explosives, expect to be caught out one day and Colton Jeffrey is about to discover the consequences of interfering in something he should have left well alone.

Then there's his sister. Currently my guest locked in the room I had made ready for her. A softer approach was needed because it was obvious she was never going to give me what I wanted under pressure. Part of me admires her for that and part of me is disappointed she caved in out of greed. I dangled a gold-plated carrot before her and she reached out and swallowed it whole. She belongs to me now because she sold her soul to me in that one act of greed and now she's going to regret every word she wrote in that journal by the time I've finished with her.

A knock on the door interrupts my maniacal thoughts and Sam enters looking like hell, which makes me smile.

"Bad night."

"I wasn't aware the day had ended."

He groans as he runs his hand through his hair and looks as if he could do with an intravenous drip of coffee to get him through the day.

"We went through the apartment, her paperwork, her computer files, anything we could think of and there is no record of her stepbrother anywhere."

Sam sighs and slumps into the seat opposite my desk. "So, he's a ghost."

"Apparently so. Any trace of him has been wiped from existence, which makes me think we're dealing with a professional."

"He doesn't want to be found. I can understand why."

"Did you find anything in her journal?"

"Nothing I want repeated."

"It's that bad then."

"Worse." Sighing, I lean back and for a moment we stare at each other under the realization for once in our lives we are not in control of a situation.

I can only hope that Ryder has a better system than ours and finds the bastard because until we do, we're fucked.

"What about Miss. Bryant? Do you think she knows?"

Thinking about the woman who has written her way into a shit load of trouble, I feel strangely excited to watch her unravel.

"I think she's being used. Probably knows nothing but what he's fed her. I'm guessing she knows shit about his where-abouts, but she could be our only hope of discovering where that is."

"What's your plan?"

"Extract the information until we find what we're looking for. She's currently my newest employee and eager to succeed. I'm guessing I can manipulate that to my advantage and use her to trap her stepbrother into making a mistake."

"She's all you've got then, because there's shit in her apart-ment. The woman's a machine. No friends, no social life, just a desire to succeed. Even her co-workers know shit about her because she kept herself apart from them and didn't get involved in the usual office politics."

"Impressive, she's driven, I like that."

Sam nods. "Yes, she sounds a lot like you. Why wouldn't you?"

He yawns loudly and I sigh. "Get some sleep, Sam, you've earned it. Leave Miss. Bryant to me. I'll see what I can screw from her."

Sam shakes his head and almost staggers to his feet. "I'm not going to argue with you. The only thing I'm interested in right now is my bed."

As he leaves, I feel bad that I've worked him so hard. He's been up all night with Scott and Michael searching her apartment and reading through her records. Three men who I keep close and pay well for the privilege. The men who do my dirty work and I would trust with my life. I have a feeling that's at stake now, along with potentially four of my friends and the clock is ticking because Ryder's right, we don't have long before we all meet up for the first time in history in a little under two weeks' time. We have a wedding to attend and everything is pointing to an extremely unwelcome visitor making an appearance.

As I HEAD toward Holly's room, I wonder if she knows already. I'm guessing waking up after the day she had yesterday would have thrown up a few surprises, and I wonder how she'll deal with knowing we have searched her apartment and gone through her private things. Angry, I'm guessing, afraid even, but she's not stupid and will know I read that journal because that's exactly what I need her to know. I want her to be afraid, so afraid right now because her fear is going to get me what I want in more ways than one.

Taking the key from my pocket, I prepare myself for a verbal onslaught, possibly a physical one, as I turn it and step into the room. Once again, I'm surprised to see her standing at the window looking out over the grounds, seemingly lost in thought. She looks impressive with her summer dress clinging to her tiny waist and spilling over those generous hips. Her dark hair is brushed long and gleams as it touches the small of her back and she appears pensive and a little lost as she says in a soft voice that throws me a little, "So now you know."

"Know what?"

Closing the door behind me, I lean against it and she sighs. "If it's worth anything, I'm sorry."

I wasn't expecting this and try not to let the surprise show in my words as I say abruptly, "Sorry for what?"

Turning, she looks directly at me and it touches me in a place I forgot existed—my heart because she looks so sorrowful. Like a painting that would hang in the finest gallery titled 'regret' because this woman is struggling to deal with her part in this.

Is it regret she was discovered, or regret that she never got to see it through? Possibly regret that she's standing there now and I expect fear that her career is over before it really got off the ground.

"I'm sorry for you."

"Why?"

"Because of what happened in your past."

I feel sick right now as she uses my weakness against me in a direct hit and I never saw it coming. Everything I try to forget is rushing back with a vengeance and I thank God I'm leaning against the wall right now because I have lost control of my muscles.

She turns and the look she gives me shocks me more than anything because she looks so worried, compassionate even, and I can't deal with it.

Reverting to the only defense I have, I snarl. "I don't want your pity. I don't want anything from you except the whereabouts of your stepbrother, so cut the emotional crap and give me everything you know."

"You already have it."

Her eyes flash as a little of her spark returns and she hisses. "You know it all because apparently you broke into my apartment, went through all my personal stuff, stole it along with me and kept me imprisoned here overnight, while you trashed my past and present. You could have asked; I would have been more than willing to help if you have asked nicely, but no. You reverted to type and took what you wanted without any thought of how I would feel about this. You're a bastard, Dexter, a cold, calculating, bastard and you can't even accept my apology like a man."

For some reason I laugh, which only annoys her more, and she hisses, "Do you think this is funny, Mr. Prince, because you're the only one laughing. You broke me yesterday. You humiliated me, stripped me of everything and made me fear for my life. You took the information I gave you, but that just wasn't enough. You want the whole of me and I still don't understand why. Yes, I wrote a story about your friend. Big deal, shit happens. You've done far worse and at least nobody died because of it."

She's gone too far, and she knows it, judging by the look of horror in her eyes as she steps back. Maybe it's the murderous look on my face, or the darkening atmosphere in the room because suddenly she has given me exactly what I want. A license to destroy because she just signed her own death warrant.

CHAPTER 14

HOLLY

I've gone way too far. Just the look on his face tells me that as clear as anything. He looks absolutely furious, and the tortured look in his eyes tells me I'm a grade A fool. I've prodded the beast and he's about to strike.

In a matter of seconds, he crosses the room and looms before me like a vengeful demon. His eyes flash and the hard look in them makes me weak at the knees and not for the reason I thought it would. He is sending a carnal message straight to my core and far from feeling afraid right now, all I feel is desire in its most destructive form.

He reaches out and grabs my wrist hard, and the pain that shoots through me is not unpleasant. Pushing me forcibly against the wall, he holds his hand to my throat and presses in and I see the madness dancing in his eyes as he hisses, "You know fuck about me, Holly Bryant. If you did, you would never have allowed those words to pass your lips. I never had you down as a fool, misguided perhaps, ambitious even, but never a fool. Well, I was wrong because you have just changed the game and you don't even know it."

I try so hard to draw myself up to his level, which is impossible. My usual bravado deserts me as I hold my breath and wait to see where this is leading. Will he kill me right now? Close those fingers around my throat and squeeze the life from inside me? Or will he rough me up a bit, teach me a lesson and cause me physical pain in return for the mental one he is experiencing right now?

He looks at me as if he's sizing up his options. Calculating, hard and dominant. All man and it surrounds him like a tangible force.

I stare at him with a mixture of desire and horror as he pulls me up effortlessly against the wall and holds me there so my feet are dancing in mid-air.

I almost can't breathe and feel the fumes of destiny stripping the air from my lungs as he holds me like a puppet suspended in uncertainty.

Then he surprises me by crushing his lips to mine in a frenzied attack. Biting, punishing and drawing blood like the most depraved of vampires. He holds me against the wall, punishing, brutal and dominant, and a feeling of such desire washes through my body that has absolutely no reason being there.

I hate that I'm loving this.

I hate that I'm craving it.

I hate that I return his kiss like a woman desperate for whatever this cruel man can give me, and I hate that I am surrounded by insanity as I kiss him back with everything I've got.

With a groan, he pushes in hard and knocks the air from my lungs as my legs wrap around his waist and I cling on tight.

He is savage, brutal and so sexy it hurts my heart because I want this so badly. I want *him* so badly and as he twists those destructive hands in my hair and pulls down hard, I cry out with a mixture of pain and ecstasy.

That shocks me more than anything because I don't do

rough love. I don't do rough anything and yet he is unleashing a monster that has remained well hidden until now.

I moan as he bites my neck and feel the wet slick of my own betrayal coating my drenched pussy. Wrapping it in infernal lust and desire for something that has been building since I first set eyes on him only yesterday morning. I want him. I want him to fuck me raw and ruin me forever because Dexter Prince is a god among men that women like me don't have a pass to.

Before I can even draw breath, he lifts me in his arms and pulls me across his lap on the bed and tears down those sodden panties and strikes a blow so painful, I bite my lip to deal with the pain. The sharp slap reverberates around the room and I cry out in shock and mortification.

He doesn't stop either and rains blows of retribution down on my ass until the tears soak the comforter, which is against the trade descriptions act because the last thing I'm feeling right now is comfort.

He has humiliated me again. Over and over again, and any desire I have for him has been replaced with anger and disgust. The disgust I'm feeling, however, is directed more at myself because I hate that I'm loving every minute of this. It's him. The man. The Monster. Somehow any form of contact with him is welcomed with need and I'm not sure where it came from.

I want him so badly. The powerful, dominant, crazy man who has made me his number one priority right now and not in a good way. What has happened to me?

I think my mind shifts into survival mode and I just shut down while he punishes me in the most humiliating of ways.

When he stops, he stands abruptly and I fall to a heap on the floor, crying, tortured and ashamed as my heart beats erratically and I feel the loss of him already. I almost expect him to kick me to finish the job, but he just says angrily, "Clean yourself up and report to me in my den. Lesson one, never use my past as a weapon. You won't like what happens next."

Before I can even catch my breath, he is gone, the door slamming behind him as the final blow and as I hear his footsteps walking away from me, I curl up into a ball and cry a river of tears because more than anything, I can't bear that he's gone.

CHAPTER 15

DEXTER

I lost it. The control that I pride myself on deserted me in seconds when she used my past mistake against me. I couldn't control the beast that lies within me, mainly dormant, but pounced as soon as she rattled his cage. I wanted to kill her, but above all I wanted to fuck her into submission. She doesn't get to talk back to me, nobody does, and it's that part of me I struggle to control. It's why I pay women for sex. They don't challenge me; they don't want to get inside my head and they don't answer back. Then Holly arrived and doesn't appear to have read the instructions on the box. I saw red and proved to myself I need help and fast.

I'm ashamed that I left her in a crumpled heap on the floor with harsh words ringing in her ears. This isn't me. I'm not an animal who treats women like trash, but she prodded a memory I haven't come to terms with yet.

I head straight to my den to wait for her to show and I wouldn't blame her if she tried to escape. How can anyone think what just happened is ok? She will hate me and deservedly so.

Pouring myself a stiff whiskey as soon as I slam the door

shut, I stare broodingly out of the window, wondering when I turned into the person I have been for some time now.

I've always been a dominant even before events spiraled out of control, but somehow my humanity was lost in the aftermath of what happened when I broke my own rules.

As I sit pondering a past that hasn't been left behind, I try so hard to get it under control.

It must be only thirty minutes later that a gentle tap on the door breaks my concentration and as the door opens, I see the woman herself venture timidly inside.

She looks down at the ground and appears to be loathing every minute of this, and I hate that I've already chipped away a little of her strength.

"Sit down."

My voice is curt and dead to my own ears and she nods before taking the chair before me and looking down, her hands trembling in her lap as she struggles to breathe the same air as me.

Pouring her a glass of the hard stuff, I slide it across the desk and say abruptly, "You may need this. It will help."

She winces as she moves and I know she is feeling the burn of my anger on her ass and I breathe out with a mixture of satisfaction and anger at myself. I hurt her and in doing so I hurt myself because I use pain to give pleasure and I kind of forgot the pleasure part in my anger.

"So, your job, maybe we should run through a few things before we start."

She looks up in surprise. "I still have one then."

"Of course, nothing has changed I'm a man of my word."

"But how…"

"You think what happened back there changes things?"

She nods miserably.

"Not on my side, although you may think differently now. What's it to be, Holly, push aside your feelings and grab this once in a lifetime opportunity, or turn and walk away because you can't deal with what just happened?"

I watch with interest as she appears to be struggling with her own demons. Of course she wants this position. She doesn't have much of a choice, really. She was fired for misconduct and any reference she seeks would assure she never gets any job she applies for, anyway. She's finished in journalism and she knows it, yet what I just did doesn't sit well with her. Hell, it doesn't sit well with me either and I wonder if she can push her hatred aside and rise above it because if she wants to succeed in this business, she will need to develop that particular skill as a matter of priority.

She exhales sharply and looks me directly in the eye with a look of pure hatred and I resist a smile breaking out because there she is, the woman that caught my interest the moment she called me sir.

"I have no choice and you know it."

"That's true, but in life we all have choices determined by what we want the most. Nobody is forcing you to take this job, Holly. You are a free woman and can make your own decisions."

I'm surprised when she laughs harshly. "So I'm free now, then why doesn't it look like that from where I'm sitting?"

I raise my glass to her and laugh softly. "Agreed. You make a fair point, but you *will* be free. When we locate your stepbrother and discover what he's up to, you will be free to carry on with your life. Until then, you can make use of the situation you have fallen into and learn a valuable lesson."

"From you." She raises her eyes and I nod.

"Yes, from me. It's just up to you how far you want to go with what I can teach you."

"What's that supposed to mean?"

She speaks with words outlined in steel and I physically ache to break her down; to see her look at me with desire and crave what I can give her. Images of her on her knees waiting for instruction fill my mind and just the thought of her naked is doing strange things to my reasoning. For some reason, I want the whole of her. Her body, her mind and her submission because I want to play with this shiny new toy and teach her just how amazing life can be when it's controlled by someone with your best interests at heart. It shocks me that she's the one. I wasn't even aware I was searching for her until that word struck me deep in the soul.

Sir.

It's like she was coming home—to me. As if somewhere in a past life we met before and were always meant to be together. I have a primal need to control every part of her and what happened back in that bedroom was just the start of something I am impatient to begin, so I do something completely out of character and lean forward and say firmly, "Look at me."

She raises those gorgeous brown eyes to mine and I see the uncertainty in them as I say, "I have an offer you may want to consider that, shall we say, is a little unorthodox."

"Go on." She looks nervous but interested, and I take that as a sign to push on with my mad proposal.

"Holly, I am looking for someone to fill another type of job role, something a little more personal."

"I see. What does it involve?"

She looks mildly curious and I raise the glass of whiskey to my lips, needing the courage it gives me before mine deserts me. "The job offer as my apprentice still stands. The contract is being drawn up as we speak and the salary negotiable."

"And." Her eyes are now bright with interest and I wonder how she'll look when my next sentences register.

"Do you know what a dominant is, Holly?"

"Maybe you should explain." She is giving nothing away and

75

I can't read her, so I carry on regardless, just hoping she's not completely freaked out by what I'm about to say.

"I like to dominate women—sexually."

She holds up her hand and says quickly, "Just stop right there, Mr. Prince, because if you are about to say what I think you are, the answer is no."

The disappointment hits me harder than I thought and I raise my eyes. "You haven't heard the facts yet, aren't you being a little hasty?"

"I *feel* the facts, Mr. Prince, that you so kindly wrote with the palm of your hand on my ass. If you think I enjoyed that, you are wrong. You may get gratification at beating a woman into submission but quite frankly it did nothing for me, so keep your second job offer to yourself and re advertise because I'm not interested in applying."

The spark in her eyes excites me even further, and yet I have to respect her decision and just shrug. "Fine, have it your way and we'll revisit this conversation when you've had time to think it over."

"I already have, the answer is no." She looks in two minds whether to say anything and then obviously decides she can't keep it in and says angrily, "The only thing that interests me about you, Mr. Prince, is your knowledge. I want to be the best journalist I can possibly be and despite how I feel about you as a person, you are the best in the business. So, I will push aside your, quite frankly, disgusting treatment of me so far and accept the apprentice job, but that is all. Lay one hand on me again and I'll report you to the cops for assault. Don't think I won't either because I am so done with playing the victim here and if you don't like it, let me go and you will never see me again."

To my surprise, she stands and says firmly, "Now, if you'll excuse me, I need something to eat, so maybe you can send me the contract to read over before I sign. I'll be in my prison and before you tell me otherwise, remember I didn't ask for any of this and need some time to myself to adjust to what happened. You have what you wanted—the name of my informant, don't make me regret giving it to you."

Without another word, she turns and leaves my office and if I feel anything at all, it's that now I want her even more.

CHAPTER 16

HOLLY

$\mathcal{I}$ am fuming. More than fuming, I'm apoplectic with rage. The bastard, the cock-sucking traitorous bastard. How dare he beat my ass and then ask me to be his fuck toy? The man's a monster of the highest caliber and I am so not going to play the victim.

I am an educated woman who has moved mountains to get that job in Media Corp, and I did it without sleeping my way through the door. I would hate myself as much as I hate him right now because I am *not* a woman like that.

You're a fool.

That bitch inside my head shouts me down as I struggle to get my rage under control. I carry on walking, wishing I could shed that part of me that is more than interested in his proposition. Be his—intimately.

Part of me is running to sign the contract already because I have never met a more attractive man in my life. It's not just that super-sexy appearance either, it's him. The man himself. He exudes power and authority, and his lazy drawl sends shivers down my spine. He's ultra-sexy in a soul shredding way and I absolutely cannot let him into my heart because I kind of need it to survive and I know this all just a game to him.

He wants me—for sex and that is all. Not me. Not Holly Bryant, who has a personality hidden somewhere behind the freakish body nature delivered on a drunk day at the office. I deserve more. I *demand* more and if that bastard wants to get anywhere near me intimately, he can work for it, because I value my dignity way more than his fucking ego.

Somehow, I find my way to the kitchen, probably due to the smell of freshly baked bread wafting my way like the gingerbread house in Hansel and Gretel. I certainly feel as if I've stumbled into a wicked fairy story because that man is evil personified.

The kind smile of his housekeeper, soothes my anger a little and the worried frown that darkens her face tells me I'm allowing my emotions to show.

"Hey, honey, come in and I'll pour you a coffee. I can add a brandy to it if you like, you look as if you need it."

"I'm good, thanks."

Somehow, I manage to raise a smile and as I sit, my mouth waters at the freshly baked bread in a basket on the table beside fresh fruit and cinnamon rolls.

"Can I cook you something, honey, eggs, bacon perhaps, what about pancakes, just name it and I'll whisk it up?"

"All of the above."

I laugh as she grins and high fives me. "That's my girl, music to my ears."

I watch as she drags out the skillet and expertly cracks some eggs into it, and soon the smell of frying eggs and bacon makes my stomach growl.

By the time it's sitting on a plate before me, I feel a little better about my situation. I stood up to the beast, and I survived—for now, anyway.

Maisy takes the seat opposite me and shakes her head. "I'm guessing Dexter played his cards all wrong as always."

"What makes you say that?" I roll my eyes and she laughs. "Man, that guy is certainly hot and successful in every way but he has a lot to learn about women."

Wondering if she is speaking from experience, she sighs. "In all the years I've been here with Jason, I've never seen him with a woman. Word is, he keeps them away because he's not interested. When I heard you were here, it gave me hope until I learned the reason for it and I can't even begin to tell you how mad that made me."

She shakes her head and sips her coffee. "But all that aside, he's a good guy, one of the best. Whatever his reason for bringing you here must be a good one, because that man has a heart of gold inside that perfect body. He just lacks experience with women."

I almost spit out my food and she giggles as I wipe the tears from my eyes. "Ok, bad choice of words, because I'm guessing that man could teach us all a thing or two, but emotions, well, he doesn't have any, so that's why whatever's happened, don't take it personally. He needs a strong woman to show him how it's supposed to be done."

"Then I wish her luck."

I chew on my food thoughtfully and then say, "You know, Maisy, that man could have it all if he just learned the right way to go about things. He thinks he can just click his fingers and get what he wants with no effort on his part at all. Looks count for a lot, but it's what's inside that matters. He may look amazing but his personality sucks—big time."

For a moment we just giggle and then somebody enters the room who makes my jaw drop because he is all man, right here dressed like a cowboy looking at Maisy as if he wants to eat her alive.

"Hey, baby, have you met Holly?"

She smiles at him and I realize this must be her husband.

"No, Darlin', I haven't had the pleasure. Good to see you out and about."

He winks and drops a sexy kiss on Maisy's willing lips and I feel a sharp pain as I realize this is what I want. The mutual love and respect. To be part of a couple who complete the picture. Equals, friends, lovers and soul mates. Not some business arrangement based on sex. I'm not that woman and I never will be.

Maisy dishes him up some food and I feel a little in the way, so make my excuses and head back to my room.

Today is going to be interesting because I never know what to expect next and if anything, Dexter Prince intrigues me way more than I'm happy to admit.

As soon as I step into the room, though, I freeze on the spot because sitting waiting for me in a seat by the window is the man himself.

His sharp stare penetrates my soul and I swallow hard because he looks pissed and I'm guessing it's because I didn't agree to his plan.

Before him on the small table is a set of papers and a pen and he says sharply, "Your contract. Sit and we'll run through it."

Taking a seat on the edge of the bed, I try hard to regain some kind of professionalism.

"That was quick."

I stare him right in the eye and he shrugs. "I had it drawn up last night. All it took was an email and a printer and here we are."

"Yes, um, here we are."

It hasn't escaped my notice that we are in a bedroom and thinking of the type of contract he had in store for me makes me a little anxious and he smirks as he lifts the first page.

"It's all set out, your terms of employment, duties, salary, leave entitlement, the lot. Sign this and you become my apprentice and just for the record, I won't be going easy on you. If you want to learn this business, then you had better be prepared for what that involves. I'm a bastard, a hard boss and I don't have time for stupid questions, or people who expect to have a life outside of the office. Sign this and you're mine until I say otherwise."

He hands me the pen and I make no move to reach it. He raises his eyes and I say firmly, "I will read it properly before signing anything. And for the record, you don't own me and you never will. I will work hard but will leave when I say so. You may have imprisoned me once, but never again. You see, you owe *me*, Mr. Prince, not the other way around because so far you have broken every rule in employment law and some criminal ones. So, you will teach me how to be the best and I will learn, but I will not be bullied by you. Do I make myself clear?"

I almost close my eyes as I wait for the storm to hit and am surprised when a low chuckle reaches my ears instead. "Understood, Miss. Bryant. I'm guessing I kind of deserved that. Fine, take your time, read the contract and then bring it to my office signed or unsigned, the choice is yours. Just so you know, for future reference, this is the only contract I expect you to honor. There is no other offer on the table so you can relax knowing I am no longer interested."

He puts the pen down and stands and as he passes me, his aftershave wraps me in pleasure because God help me, now he has backed away, I want him even more.

CHAPTER 17

DEXTER

I leave Holly to read through the contract and retreat to my den to get some actual work done. When she turned me down, it hurt my ego, but when I had time to think, I admire her spunk. She has gone way higher in my estimation and if anything, I want her even more, but the game has now changed and I am no longer interested in dominating her. For some reason, she doesn't fit the profile of a submissive, but she does interest me in another way.

When she said 'no' it was a declaration of war because now the game has changed and it has become even more important to me to claim this woman as mine and then get on with my life. The challenge has been set and I'm up for it, so God help the delectable Miss. Bryant, because I always get what I want and she will be begging me to change my mind and offer her the position in my bed.

For the next hour, I throw myself into my work. It always calms me and brings me back from the edge, and it always has. I love what I do and somehow interfering in other people's lives and reporting on news, distracts me from the mess I have made of my life so far.

Thinking about the mess I've made of Holly's life so far fills me with regret because she doesn't deserve what's happening right now. The trouble is, this is out of control and none of us count in the grand scheme of things. I reassure myself that we must do whatever it takes to protect our organization, even though somebody may be tearing it apart from the inside out.

Thinking back on the time I learned of it, I wonder that it didn't drive me crazy. Sometimes I think how lucky I was to fall into this life, other times I feel like the unluckiest bastard alive. I wonder what Travis Peters would do now in my position? He was an insufferable bastard who mentored me, much like I offered Holly, but I never understood the real reason behind his offer. When he died, the baton was handed to me and I almost screwed it up. I forgot the golden rule of journalism and have spent the past five years paying for it.

Will I make that mistake again with Holly? That's the part scaring me the most, because when she discovers what we've done, she may never talk to me again. In fact, she may do something we both regret, and I'm not sure I'm ready for that.

The door opens and this time she doesn't even knock and strides into my office as if she owns it. She has changed from the simple sun dress into a business suit that makes my mouth water. The short sexy skirt that dusts the skin just above the knees is tempting to the extreme. Her tight fitted shirt strains to contain breasts that have their own identity that dance before my eyes and the smart jacket completes a look that means business and yet distracts any red-blooded male into thinking depraved thoughts and desiring the woman who apparently couldn't give a shit.

Her long dark hair has been pulled into a severe pony tail that only intensifies her features as the make-up she has used defines her perfect face. Those dark brown eyes flash as she drops the contract down on my desk and says abruptly, "I have signed your contract because I want to learn. I want to be the best, Mr. Prince, and I am counting on you to honor your promise. I will work hard, listen and be the best apprentice you ever had."

"That's not difficult."

"What isn't?"

"Being the best apprentice I've ever had because darlin', you're the *only* apprentice I've ever, um, had, and so the bar is set very low. It's up to you to raise it to a level the next person can't reach. Do you think you're up to that?"

"Of course."

"Then we start now."

She looks excited and I see the fire in her eyes and I love seeing it burn a little brighter when I say casually, "Coffee, now."

For a moment she looks uncertain, as if she misheard me and I snap, "I said coffee, Holly, don't you understand the most basic of requests?"

"But I thought…" She seems genuinely confused and I smirk. "You're an apprentice, Holly, not some super executive. You start at the bottom and prove your worth, and that begins with making me coffee. I like it strong black and the water at boiling point. Maisy will show you how, and I expect to see it here on the dot of seven every morning and then at two-hourly intervals throughout the day. I also expect you to have a list of my appointments, meetings and any documents needed made ready for me that Helen, my assistant, sends over the night before. Once we leave and begin working at Media Corp, you must liaise with her because she is your new best friend and between you make sure my machine is well-oiled and running smoothly."

"Is that it?"

"I think so - for now."

"But I thought…"

"I know what you thought, Holly. You thought you had a

one-way ticket to the top. You thought you had a chance to start where most people spend a lifetime aiming for. Sorry to be the bearer of bad news but you've just signed your life away to me and you have to earn this opportunity in a far more demanding way than most. So get the coffee, shut your mouth and do what the hell I tell you and then maybe we can get on with our extremely busy day."

For a moment I think she's going to stab me with my letter opener but instead she just throws me a disgusted look and storms from my office without a backward glance, leaving me grinning like a fucking idiot. Just imagining the pleasure it will give me breaking her down is giving me a little light relief because one thing's for sure, Holly Bryant will be mine in every way possible by the end of this extremely interesting experiment.

CHAPTER 18

HOLLY

I might have known. I may have been offered the opportunity of a lifetime, but it's with the Devil himself. Just the smirk on his face as he promised he wasn't going to make it easy on me told me everything I needed to know. But I want this. More than anything it seems, but part of me still regrets selling out my family for personal gain.

I wonder if Colton knows. He will be surprised the article never found its way to the public. He will be wondering what happened and is probably trying to contact me.

Just thinking about the circumstances that led me here makes me even more confused than ever.

I thought he was helping me. Had information that would make my career fly. I would be that journalist who sniffs out a story and exposes the truth. A hard-hitting woman who is better than any of the men further up the ladder than me.

I still don't understand what was so damning about it. As articles go, it was quite tame, really. There is definitely more than meets the eye about this whole fiasco and now I'm in the prime position to find out exactly what that is.

Once the coffee is made, I head back and see Dexter hard at

work and something stirs emotion inside me. Just watching the great man at work is a pleasure because his reputation is one of a demigod. I must push aside my hatred of the man to learn from the master and so I set the coffee down and say expectantly, "Can I help?"

He raises those sinful eyes to mine and the look in them makes me swoon. He is so sexy it blinds me to his faults, and when he directs that powerful gaze at me with a mixture of lust and an obscene amount of interest, it's a hard situation to be in. He makes no secret that he wants me and it's taking all my acting skills to pretend I'm not interested. But I am. Far too interested for my own good and the excitement I feel when I'm around him has nothing to do with the apprenticeship. It's like unfinished business of the most depraved kind, and I think we both know where this will end.

"I need you to do some digging on a Jefferson Powers."

"What, the oil baron?"

"Yes. Rumor has it he's drowning in debt and trying to stay afloat. His shareholders are antsy and to make matters worse, his wife is having an affair with his closest rival."

"Wow." I can feel my eyes shining as I sense a story that will run for weeks and make Media Corp a lot of money in the process.

Dexter smirks arrogantly, "Remember to deal with the facts, Holly. This story will ruin lives and you need to have every fact backed up three-fold."

"Of course."

He raises his eyes and I blush when I remember the reason I'm here. Did I trust the wrong man? Was Colton feeding me a lie, and I foolishly published without knowing the facts.

Almost as if he can read minds, Dexter says in a strangely gentle voice, "You weren't to know."

For some reason, his kindness hits me harder than I thought and I nod, not really knowing what to say because apparently, I did get it wrong and he was right to pull the story.

"Holly, we've all made mistakes, it's up to us to learn from them. It makes us better because those mistakes make us stronger."

"It doesn't make me feel better though, I'm just glad you stopped it in time."

To my surprise, he shakes his head and says almost regretfully, "I wish somebody had stopped me."

"What happened?" I hold my breath because Dexter is opening up to me in the most surprising of ways and I like what I see. The more vulnerable side to a powerful man makes him almost appear human.

"Maybe I'll tell you the full story when I can trust you with the facts."

He grins to take the edge from his words and then waves toward a desk set up in the corner of the room.

"There's a computer waiting to use in your investigation. I've had everything I could find on Jefferson, his wife and the company loaded onto it, and I need you to sift through it all and highlight anything of interest. It's a tedious job, but you've got to start somewhere. Put your findings in a report and get it back to me by close of business today.

"Of course, sir. You can rely on me."

The look in his eyes surprises me. For some reason, he winced when I called him sir and it confuses me. Doesn't he like it, I know he asked me to call him Dexter and maybe he is angry I didn't use his name?

"Do you have anything to say, Holly?"

He looks amused and I shake my head, "No, I'm sorry, I'll get right on it."

Taking my seat, I feel a rush of excitement that tells me I did the right thing. This is pure gold. To be trusted with forming a story that will blow the wires into space. This is what I trained so hard for, this buzz of excitement in uncovering the truth and exposing people who should know better.

I am so absorbed in the life of Jefferson Powers, I don't even notice how many hours have passed until Dexter stands behind me and snaps the laptop lid closed. "What?"

"Lunch." He smirks as he reaches out and takes my hand, pulling me up and away from my work.

Just feeling his hand in mine is like an electric shock and as those deep, dark eyes bore into mine, a shiver passes through me as his aftershave wafts around my soul.

"Come, Maisy makes amazing club sandwiches. You must be hungry."

"I suppose I am." I laugh softly because the past few hours could have been minutes as far as I'm concerned, and I suddenly realize I'm hungry and desperate for a drink.

Dexter seems quite mellow for once and as we walk toward the kitchen, I decide to capitalize on that and say slightly nervously, "Have you located my stepbrother?"

"Not yet."

He carries on and I say lightly, "I could help."

"No, you can't."

"But why, surely, I'm your best chance at finding him? I mean, if he's in danger, I want you to find him and keep him safe."

"Why?"

"What do you mean, why? He's family."

Dexter stops suddenly and I'm surprised when his eyes flash and he snarls, "Family who sacrifices their sister for personal gain. He didn't have your best interests at heart, Holly. He was using you and so you don't need to feel guilty about giving us his name."

"What do you mean?" I'm fearful of his answer and he snarls, "Colton is working for somebody we need to find. There is no possible way he could have discovered that information without being fed it by an unknown source. He is just a puppet, and so are you. Whoever is doing this is dangerous, and it's imperative we discover his identity before it's too late."

His words silence me because suddenly I'm aware that I'm way out of my depth and from the look on his face, it could ruin us both.

CHAPTER 19

DEXTER

*H*olly impresses me more with every day that goes by. She's a fast learner and anything I ask her to do is done with speed and accuracy. She is determined to excel at whatever task I set her, and I have grown accustomed to her being by my side.

For the most part, our relationship is purely professional and I'm longing to change that because just breathing the same air as her is interfering with my rational mind.

My days are spent resisting my primal urges where she's concerned and my nights spent jerking off like a high school jock desperate for sex.

I'm in an intolerable situation and something has to give before I go insane.

We are working in my den as usual, and Holly sighs and lowers her laptop lid.

"Is there a problem?"

I look at her sharply and she shakes her head. "I could really do with some fresh air, if I'm honest. I've been here already for the best part of a week and haven't even seen the sunrise."

"Do you make a habit of that?"

"Every day."

She looks a little lost as she says softly, "When I was growing up, I was shipped from one boarding school to another. It wasn't a happy time and I never really fitted in. The only pleasure I got was to get up early and go for a jog, ending up on the ridge above the school and watching the sunrise. I always wished on that sun signifying the new day."

"What did you wish for?"

"A different life. One where I wasn't under someone else's control, able to make my own decisions and do what was right for me."

I choose my words carefully. "Control can be liberating if placed in the right hands."

She spins on her seat and looks at me from under those long, dark lashes, with a mixture of curiosity and fear.

"How?"

"I could show you but I don't think you're ready."

I hold my breath because this could just be the break I need and she says shyly, "I'd like to know more."

Putting my pen down, I stand and note the interest in her eyes as I walk toward her. Crouching down before her, I take her hand and love how soft it feels in mine.

Her breathing is irregular and her eyes are bright and I say huskily, "If you place your trust in one person one hundred percent, it can be a beautiful experience. Somebody who places your interests above their own and will do anything to make things right for you. In return, you relinquish control and trust them completely. Only then do you benefit from the full experience."

"That sounds—scary."

I see the doubt in her eyes but she's interested, that's obvious and I stroke the back of her hand, loving the shiver that passes through her as her eyes burn with lust.

"I can't give you the sunrise, Holly, not yet, anyway, but I can give you a different kind of freedom."

"What do you mean, surely I can watch the sunrise?"

"There's something you should know first."

I'm not sure if this is such a good idea but it would have come out sooner or later and pulling her up, I guide her to the couch and sit beside her, my hand in hers.

"The reason you're here is to remove you from life."

"What does that mean?"

She sounds fearful and bit guarded and I sigh. "The whole scene back at Media Corp was engineered for a very good reason. Everybody needed to see you lose your job in a humiliating way."

"Why, it doesn't make sense?"

She looks angry and I say bitterly. "I'm sorry, Holly. It was exactly the right thing to do. The fact your entire apartment was shipped here that same day and that you were stripped of all communications was to make you disappear. We need Colton to fear for your life in order to flush him out of whatever sewer he's in."

"Then you've wasted your time." She laughs bitterly. "Colton doesn't care for me; he wouldn't give a fuck."

"Maybe not, but surely even your stepbrother would show up to your funeral."

"Oh my God, what?"

She starts to shake and I place my arm around her shoulders and pull her tightly against me and stroke her hair as I whisper, "The headlines the next day reported you as missing. Rumor was created that you took off when your career ended. Various reports from fabricated sources speak of you being suicidal, crazy even and I'm sorry to say presumed dead."

She pulls away and says in shock, "You killed me, why?"

"To flush out the person responsible for putting you here. As we speak, your father has returned from the Middle East and you stepmother is dining out on tearful interviews about how devastated she is. We are watching their every move and monitoring their phones. If Colton shows his face, we've got him, and then you can miraculously reappear and explain it as a vacation. We have your story ready and make it check out so now you can see why I need to keep you inside. If anyone is watching this place, or monitoring our communications, your cover would be blown."

She falls silent and I can tell she's struggling. I watch as she plays with her fingers as the emotional part of her deals with the pragmatic part. Holly will know this is the best way to discover her stepbrother's whereabouts, but she's no fool and says icily, "Why didn't you let me help? I could have arranged to meet him, find out what he knows. You didn't need to trash my reputation and make me look crazy."

"I'm sorry, baby, we did. There was no other way because your brother is somehow manipulating our communications. Whoever he is working for is always one step ahead of us and pulling our strings. This gives us the element of surprise and until we have him under lock and key, none of us are safe."

"I've just got your word on that; how do I know you're telling the truth?"

"You don't, you just have to learn to trust me, Holly and like I said, I don't think you're ready for that."

She stands and says tightly, "If you'll excuse me, I need some time to think about this."

"Of course, take as long as you need, but know that what-ever happens, I have your best interests at heart. I'm not about to break another person in my exposure of the truth, so can you trust me Holly?"

She looks a little surprised and curious and then says, "Maybe I can trust you if you earn that trust. Be open with me, Dexter, let me in a little and let me make up my own mind."

I know what she's asking, but it's impossible, so I shake my head. "Like I said, trust needs to be earned, and we are strangers. Two people balancing on the edge of something that could change us forever. Any decisions we make have consequences and they need to be the right ones, for both our sakes."

She looks as if she has something else to say but thinks better of it and just walks away. As I watch her go, I can only imagine what's running through her head right now, but if I know Holly, she will reach the right decision and that is something I'm anxious to see.

CHAPTER 20

HOLLY

*I*t's too much to take in. They've fabricated my death and involved my parents. I should be beyond angry, screaming and running for the nearest telephone to reassure them I'm ok. Strangely, I'm not.

Dexter has a way about him that makes me trust him. God only knows why, but I'm longing to see where this all ends.

Making my way toward my room, I think about the other conversation he started. Control. From the look in his eyes, I know exactly what that involves, and I'm strangely excited about that.

I see Maisy heading my way with an armful of laundry, and she smiles. "Hey, how are things?"

"Strange." I raise my eyes and she nods as if she can read my mind.

"Why don't we grab a coffee, I think we need to have a chat."

I'm surprised by the determination on her face and nod, following her to the kitchen, which always feels so homey and welcoming, probably because of the woman who lives here most of the time.

She sets about gathering the mugs and I slump down on the kitchen chair and stare into space. My mind scrambled.

The coffee she pushes my way is most welcome, and she says with interest, "I'm guessing Dexter's been messing with your mind, he's good at that."

"How did you know?" I throw her a wry smile and she leans on her elbows and looks at me curiously. "Honey, that man is a closed book. I told you that, but I'm guessing if you opened it and read the story, you would understand why."

"Do you—know the story, I mean?"

"A little, but it's not my place to tell it. Just know that Dexter is a good man. A little lost maybe and struggling to find his way. The front he puts on to the outside world is just that— a front. Underneath the hard-assed businessman is a man who feels a little too much. He is lost and I pray every night for him to find someone who can purge his demons and make him happy."

"That sounds impossible."

"No, just *almost* impossible, there's a big difference."

"But he's so cold. He brought me here and is keeping me against my will. What's right about that?"

"Are you sure?"

"Of what?"

"That you're here against your will because I've watched you both over the past few days and you have reached an understanding that tells me you're happy to be here."

"For the opportunity. I would still like my freedom and to be able to choose when I leave."

"I understand that, it's our basic human right, but, honey, as prisons go, you scored the jackpot here. Dexter is a good man and you will be well cared for. When you leave, I'm guessing he will have it all wrapped up and your life will be a much better one than the one you left."

I think about what she says and know in my heart she's

right. Dexter has been open with me to a point and I should respect him for that. Maybe the reason I'm happy to be here has more to do with the man than the job. It's the thought of spending the day with him that gets me out of bed and has me dressing in a way I think he would like. It's the little looks we share, and the stolen smiles that give meaning to my day. It's the powerful urge to massage his shoulders when he stretches wearily and my need to be close to him that surprises me more and everything he has told me just can't make me hate him. It should, but I'm excusing him every word from his lips because I want to stay, to be with him.

Now he has made me a cryptic offer that I can kind of guess what's involved and it's screwing with my head more than anything he just said. Can I trust him, relinquish control to a man who, to the outside world, is a monster? I already know my answer and that is what's exciting me the most.

Two hours later and my minds made up. I thought long and hard as I sat on my bed staring at the walls and for every reason why I should say no, there were a hundred others that told me to go for it. My life couldn't get even worse—surely and this may be something that teaches me a valuable life lesson that will benefit my future.

I head toward Dexter's den with a mixture of excitement and fear. What will happen next, it's the unknown that's scaring me a little?

I knock on the door and he says roughly, "Come in."

As I open the door, he watches me approach like a predator and I love how that makes me feel inside. One week in his company and I have lost my mind and all sense of what's right because I'm about to jump head first into a situation that could break me, or make me.

"Have you reached your decision?"

He seems mildly curious, and I lick my lips and nod.

"I have."

He looks interested and my voice shakes as I say softly, "Yes."

The spark of interest in his eyes excites me and he says carefully, "Yes to giving me control?"

"Yes." I swallow hard because now I've said it, I feel so vulnerable. I'm not even sure what I've just agreed to and as I shift nervously on my feet, he leans back and looks at me with a considered expression.

"Maybe I should tell you what's involved first. You can still say no."

"Ok."

He waves toward the seat in front of his desk and it feels like an interview for a very sick job.

My hands remain tightly clasped on my knee as I struggle to even look at him and he says firmly, "Look at me, Holly."

Raising my eyes to his, I almost jump because there's a ferociousness in his that should be scaring me right now.

The power that man surrounds himself with is a powerful aphrodisiac and I feel weak inside as he says, "The control I seek is sexual. Is that ok with you?"

I feel so mortified and feel my cheeks burn and he stares at me steadily as I lick my lips and say nervously, "I kind of guessed that."

He nods as if negotiating a business deal. "I can't promise you anything other than sexual control. Emotion is something that won't even enter our contract."

"Sex without emotion, that sounds so cold."

He shrugs. "It's for the best. I'm not promising you a love story, Holly, just a lesson in what happens when you trust someone completely to give you pleasure and take care of you. Emotion just confuses that and if at any time you want to walk away, you can."

"Can I, so if I asked to leave right now, you would let me?"

He leans back and shakes his head. "You know I can't, but

we could make your stay here count for more. In working so closely together, you will learn to trust me and understand what that means."

He leans forward and stares me straight in the eye. "Let me control you, Holly, let me show you how good that feels."

My heart rate has increased to critical levels as I nod shyly. "Ok, I'll give it a go, but only on the understanding I can back out at any time. Even if you keep me here, it must be under my terms or not at all."

The slow smile that breaks out across his devilishly handsome face makes me melt into a pool of lustful thoughts as he nods. "Agreed. Are you ready to begin?"

"What now?"

He laughs and the look he shoots me should fill me with fear but strangely only makes me desire him more.

"Yes, now, Holly. Lesson one begins now and involves stripping away any embarrassment because until you can look me in the eye, this won't work."

I swear I nearly pass out as he stands and heads my way and as he reaches for my hand, I feel as if I'm about to do something I will immediately regret but somehow want more than anything I've ever wanted before.

CHAPTER 21

DEXTER

*S*he agreed. I still can't quite believe that she did. Finally, her defenses are down and I get my wish. Cleanse her from my mind because ever since she called me sir, I have thought of little else.

Now I get everything I want and I feel like a warrior.

She shivers with expectation and I relish the sight. The moment before the point of no return and I don't know who is more nervous about this. I want to make it good for her. To show her she was right to trust me, so I take her hand and gently pull her toward me and whisper, "From now on you call me sir. I am your master and educator and you will not question me."

"Yes, sir."

Her lowered eyes and flush on her face mixed with the breathy word I desire to hear is almost unbearable and I say huskily, "We are going to have sex, Holly, it's the only way to strip away any barriers between us. Is that ok with you?"

"Yes, sir."

"Good, then follow me."

As we leave the den, I wonder what's running through her

head right now. Even my own words sound so cold, unfeeling even and yet there's a raging torrent of emotion rushing through my veins. I want this to count. I want her to share an experience unlike any she's had before and as we reach my bedroom, I can almost touch the fear surrounding her.

Stepping through the door, the large bed that greets us reinforces her position, and she falters a little and I say gently, "Remember, it's all about trust. Control and trust. I won't hurt you, Holly, I want to teach you what those words mean."

She nods and I remove my shirt, keeping my eyes on her at all times and the shiver that passes through her tells me how turned on she is, giving me the confidence I need to see this through.

"Your turn."

She looks scared shitless as she tentatively unfastens her blouse and as those glorious tits are revealed, encased in the finest lace, my cock hardens unbearably.

Unbuckling my belt, I remove it and lay it gently on the side and then keeping my eyes on her, I remove my pants and love the desire that lights in her eyes.

She follows my lead and steps out of her skirt and I feast my eyes on a body crafted for sin and a woman who would give Eve a run for her money.

Stepping forward, I unfasten her hair and allow it to spill down her back and run my fingers through the silky strands and then lowering my lips to hers, I relish our first taste as I plunge my tongue inside and wrap it around hers.

She moans and I swear it's the sweetest sound I've ever heard as she leans into me and I feel her tits graze my chest.

The fact she's still on her heels brings her almost level with me and I growl, "The heels stay."

Running my hand around the back of her, I unfasten her bra and almost groan as those tits graze my chest and gently stroke them. I love the sharp intake of breath she gives as my fingers pinch her pert nipple.

Lowering my hands, I remove the drenched panties and she gasps as she stands before me naked except for those killer heels.

Tracing her curves, I relish the sounds that I hear and her soft moans spur me on as I prepare to taste a little piece of heaven.

Whispering huskily in her ear, I say, "Today we have sex, the vanilla way. Our bodies will become accustomed to one another and then I will show you how good control can be."

She whimpers and the slick juices that coat my fingers tell me she's ready and as I lower her back onto the bed, I kiss her luscious body all over. Just imagining what I could do to this body, how I could *break* this body, sends an excitement to my cock that I haven't felt in quite some time. Not today, though. Today is all about making her feel comfortable. Making her relax with me and the easiest way for that is to love and worship her body as if she's the most desirable woman alive and, in this moment, she is. I have never wanted anyone as much as I want her and so I whisper, "Are you on birth control?"

"Yes." Her words are laced in desire and I thank God she is, because I've never been a fan of condoms, anyway. However, until I get her checked out, I would be a fool to trust that, so I reach for one anyway and say huskily, "For now, we play it safe for both our sakes."

As I sheath my rock-hard cock, I kiss her gently on the neck, chasing a trail to her amazing tits. As I suck on them, she moans and I feel like a conquering hero because her legs part and I know she is aching to feel me inside.

Continuing my feast, I head lower and she shudders as I part her wet folds and take my fill, loving how sweet she tastes. She is so ready for me it tells me I was right to force this situation and as she gasps and grabs the back of my head, I know she can't hold on much longer.

As I work my way back up her body, I gaze down at her beautiful face and feel my heart swell. Mine. My woman for as long as I say so, and that is the most potent aphrodisiac there is. My shiny new toy who I intend on playing with until I break it and she doesn't even know what she's agreed to yet went there anyway.

With one sharp move, I thrust inside and the gasp from her lips and the wonder in her eyes tells me she's ready to welcome me in and as my cock dances inside a little piece of heaven, I feel an overwhelming urge to devour her whole. A caveman disguised as a gentleman. Thrusting harder, faster and more brutally, she matches every stroke, every push and takes whatever I give her. I'm like a possessed man as I dominate this woman and show her who's in charge because now she's given me permission, I intend on doing every depraved thing in my head to this willing recipient.

She cries out and I feel her pulsating over my cock and as she screams, I know I've got her just where I want her. I pull out and she looks confused as I stand, my cock hard and unsatisfied and she says in shock, "What's wrong?"

"I told you, Holly, I'm teaching you control and you don't get the whole of me until you've earned it."

"But…"

I give her no time to think and say roughly, "On your knees."

"What, here, on the bed?"

"No, on the floor."

She looks so beautiful post orgasm, her cheeks flushed and full of pleasure, but the surprise in her eyes only enhances the image. A confused mess of lust and innocence and I fucking love it.

To her credit, she does as I ask and as I stand before her, I say firmly, "Take my cock and finish the job."

Seeing her kneeling before me is every dream I ever had as she nods and reaches for my shaft. As her lips close around it, I say huskily, "Taste yourself on my cock, Holly, does that feel good knowing you let me inside."

Her head bobs as she takes me further and I groan as she sucks noisily as I thrust in and out.

I don't hold back and thrust inside, deeper, roughly and without care, and she gags as I hit the back of her throat and gasps when I grab her hair and thrust harder. As I feel the domination, the control, it sends me wild and as I pour a steady stream of spunk down her throat, I love knowing it's coating her inside. To her credit, she finishes the job and as she licks my shaft clean, I swear I see an angel kneeling at my feet.

Pulling out, I reach for her and pull her up to meet me and as I kiss her deep and hard, I taste my own arousal on her tongue. She grinds against me and I love how she fits, as if she was always meant to be against my body.

Pushing her back onto the bed, I wrap my arms around her and hold her close and whisper, "Good girl."

Kissing the top of her head, I feel her heart beating against my chest and her breath comes quickly, telling me the emotion she's feeling right now.

As I stroke her back, I whisper, "Rest now. We'll move on tonight."

She snuggles in closer and that's all the answer I need as her even breathing tells me she's fallen into a satiated sleep.

CHAPTER 22

HOLLY

*W*hen I wake, it takes a moment to realize where I am and as the realization hits, I feel a strange mixture of emotions. I'm embarrassed to face him, yet wouldn't change what happened for a thing. It was intense, so intense, and unlike any other sexual encounter I've ever had. Maybe it was because it felt forbidden. Sex with a stranger because he is—a stranger. Sex with the boss, surely that's a taboo subject and the fact he was so commanding, was a definite turn on.

Yes, as sex goes, this one has risen to the top of the list and I am surprised that I loved it when he commanded me. It felt good to do what he asked, and seeing his happiness at what I could do made me strangely proud. Now I know I'm fucked in every way because where has this weak female come from? I pride myself on my independence. My ability to make my own rules and I hate the fact I so easily gave that away for a moment with him.

As he stirs, my heart rate increases because I'm not sure what happens next and his low, husky drawl immediately makes me wet again.

"You ok, baby?"

"Yes, um, sir."

He turns to face me and traces a path down my face toward my breasts and as I see the desire heavy in his eyes, I feel myself squirm with a need to go again.

"Ready for lesson number two?"

I nod shyly. "Ok."

He grins, showing what a cocky bastard he is, and he says roughly, "Remember, this is all about losing control to me."

"Ok."

He stands and rifles through a drawer next to his bed, and I watch with a mixture of trepidation and excitement as he removes some silk scarves.

As he sits on the bed, he says firmly, "Lie back."

I feel myself quivering with excitement as he ties my wrists to the bedposts and then secures my ankles. I should be embarrassed to be naked and spread out before him, but strangely, I'm just interested to see where this will lead. He fastens another scarf around my eyes, and it feels strangely liberating. The fact I can't see him makes it more acceptable somehow, and his voice appears as if it's from another world.

"I'm going to teach you about the senses; show you how good it can feel. It won't all be pleasure though, but you will learn to welcome the pain."

Now I'm not happy and I make to speak but as I open my mouth, he stuffs some kind of fabric inside it and whispers, "Trust me, Holly, you will love it."

My senses are on red alert as he moves off the bed and I lie rigid and disbelieving that I'm in this position at all.

The first thing I feel is something soft caressing my body, and it feels so nice and as if I'm floating on a cloud. It feels so good and soon the feather like object is replaced with his mouth and as he kisses every part of my body, I moan. I know I'm already ready to feel him inside me and I'm ashamed at how quickly he can make me want him and then I feel a shiver when he runs something cold over my breasts that almost hurts as the ice burns my skin. He replaces it with his hot mouth and it feels so good I can't stop moaning.

There is no other sound than my moans and I should be embarrassed about that, but I'm not. I want more and as he rubs some kind of lotion into my breasts, I wish he would put me out of my misery because I'm ready to explode right now.

The fact I can't see a thing, or speak, is strangely intoxicating, as if I'm not really here at all and I surround myself in fantasy as he plays my body like a maestro at the top of his game.

Then I feel the bite of leather as he flicks something hard against my abdomen and the pain causes me to jerk and a muffled scream escapes. Immediately, he runs the feather over the painful area and then kisses it softly, and the pain is replaced by ecstasy once again. Three more times he strikes, and each time is followed by a burst of pleasure that makes me welcome the pain, knowing it will end in a feeling I have yet to experience. I almost howl with disappointment when he removes the gag and unties me and as I blink in the light, I am mortified to see him sniffing my drenched panties that were apparently just in my mouth.

With a wicked grin, he tosses them into the trash can next to his bed and says darkly, "You won't be needing them again."

"What the..."

"No underwear required, because from now on, you wear what I say and allow me access whenever I choose. Your body now belongs to me, Holly, and I promise you will like how that feels."

I should be arguing right now but feel strangely turned on by it. Not knowing when he wants my body is a delicious game that I'm happy to play and so I look at him shyly and whisper, "Yes, sir."

His eyes darken at my words and I know he loves it when I address him this way and for the first time, I see the power I have over him. He wants me. Holly Bryant, insignificant junior reporter and woman without purpose. Well, I have one now and it's delighting this man who has the power to give me everything I want in life. Now I'm up for the challenge and if he wants it on his terms, bring it on.

CHAPTER 23

DEXTER

*H*olly has lived up to expectations and is a willing pupil. The fact she responded so well gives me the courage to move things on.

After we showered and changed, we went to eat and just seeing her lips wrap around the food instantly made me hard. Just imagining what I'm going to do to her makes me think of little else, and I wonder how long she'll last. My mind is depraved, sick even, and yet I can't control the urges I have to practice my craft. Because it is a craft, a study of anatomy, the female one. I have practiced well on hookers and unsuspecting dates, but I've never had my own toy to play with at will. Holly is the woman I have been waiting for and, as luck would have it, she fell into my lap in the most unusual of circumstances.

I can tell that Maisy suspects our relationship has changed. Hell, I can even feel it in the tense air myself as Holly tries desperately to keep her cool and not look me in the eye. She's embarrassed, telling me I need to break that part of her because what I have planned has no room for shame.

As soon as we finish, I take her to my library and pour us

both a couple of whiskies and say firmly, "Sit on your knees by the fireplace."

She looks a little awkward but does as I say and as she kneels, I feel the power rush when I hand her the glass and she whispers, "Thank you, sir."

Holding the glass to her lips, I grip her hands and hold them behind her and feed her the drink, staring deep into her eyes and as I pull it back, I fasten my lips to hers and love the taste of burning alcohol on her tongue. She gasps as I bite down hard and I taste the blood and without another word I feed her some more and she winces as the alcohol burns the cut.

She draws back a little and I whisper. "Relax, it only stings for a moment then feel the delicious burn inside."

She nods and I kiss her long, deep and hard until she moans against my mouth and I draw back and whisper huskily, "Take off your clothes."

"What here?" She looks anxious and I smile. "It's ok, I'll lock the door, nobody will disturb us."

Despite the fact she's unhappy about that, she does it anyway and just seeing her do what I want is a major turn on. Quickly, I lock the door and as soon as I return, I love the sight of the quivering woman shivering on the floor, kneeling before the fireplace, waiting for what I can give her. For some reason, I feel a surge of protectiveness over my student as she looks at me with misguided trust in her eyes and feel an over-whelming urge to make this right for her. To make this the best experience of her life and so I kneel before her and lightly stroke her face, looking deep into her eyes, the lamp-light casting a dancing shadow over her beautiful skin. She appears totally mesmerized as she stares back at me and as I touch her lips slightly with mine, I can taste the whiskey, fear and yet desire as she lets me take her on a journey of discovery.

The fact I'm still fully clothed is an inconvenience, but this is about her, not me, and so taking her hand, I pull her to her feet and nod to the chair in the corner of the room.

"Sit."

She does as I say and then her eyes widen as I remove my belt and say huskily, "Place your hands behind the back of the chair and clasp them tight."

The wild look in her eyes tells me she's scared but so turned on she will do anything I ask and as I secure her wrists tightly, she winces a little as the leather grazes her skin.

Leaning down, I kiss her lips hard, with a passion that excites me and causes her to groan with longing. Knowing how wet she is right now makes me feel so powerful and pulling back, I spread her legs and anchor them behind each chair leg, grabbing a couple of plastic ties from my pocket. I wink as I snap them in place and she looks a little shocked and embarrassed as she is spread out before me like the finest dessert.

Her chest heaves with excitement and a desire for what happens next and those beautiful brown eyes sparkle as she holds my stare and I feel a rush of power as I say curtly, "Are you happy, baby?"

"Yes, sir." Her answer is coy and seeing her now is a one hundred degree turn from the woman who arrived here just over a week ago. She's softer, more manageable and lacking the fire she wears so well and part of me loves that as much as I hate it too.

But how can I complain because she is doing everything I wanted and more, so I start from her perfect toes and gently suck each one into my mouth before moving up to the drenched pussy that is desperate for my attention.

As I kneel between her legs and feast on my slave, it is the sweetest feeling in the world. She doesn't know it yet, but that's exactly the role I have planned for her and this is just the start of her training. By the end of it, she will be besotted with me and do everything I ask, no matter how sick and twisted and just imagining what that means makes me harder than I've ever been. Finally, my own plaything to control and I never knew it would feel so good.

She gasps as I suck, rub and tease and as she shudders and tenses, I feel her orgasm wash over my tongue and it feeds my obsession with this woman. Her head rolls back as she shudders in the seat and I stand back and watch her come with a fascination that surprises me. It's beautiful to watch and I could play with her all day, which is exactly what I intend on doing because now I've started, it's doubtful I can stop. Like a kid with a new favorite toy, I intend on playing with it until it breaks, and that's why I'm a bastard because feelings don't come into it. Not on my part, anyway.

As she comes down from her high, I leave her tied up and move to the side table and pour us another couple of whiskies. She looks uncomfortable and wriggles a little and as I walk back, I stare at her, making her blush.

"Um, aren't you going to untie me?"

She sounds nervous and I grin wickedly, "Not yet."

"Oh."

She wets her lip and I hold the glass to them and gently pour the liquid down her throat and the flush to her cheeks makes me stop and appreciate her beauty. Sex obviously agrees with her because although she is beautiful, now she is a goddess and I stand back and openly stare, making her squirm with embarrassment.

Feeling decidedly wicked, I say roughly, "You need a lesson in trust. I am going to leave for ten minutes; you will remain like this until I return."

"What if someone comes in?" She looks worried and I shrug. "I am telling you they won't. Like I said, this is a lesson on trust. By the end of this you won't question me because every time you do, there are consequences."

"What do you mean—consequences?"

"I mean punishments, Holly. You doubt me, I punish you."

"How?" She licks her dry lips and I say in a hard voice, "Don't disobey me and you won't find out what they are. Control and trust are the only words you need to live by. Don't ever doubt my intentions toward you because they are the glue that binds us together. Betray either one of them and the whole situation becomes—painful, for both of us."

She swallows hard as the fear lights up her beautiful eyes and I say curtly, "Do you understand?"

"Yes, sir." She lowers her head and I love that she's hating this. Teaching her the basics is rewarding in so many ways and I don't stop to think about anything other than my pleasure in a situation that I couldn't have planned better if I tried, and with such an amazing woman too. To break a strong woman gives a certain kind of sweet victory and just seeing her accept the situation makes me feel invincible.

As I turn and leave the room, I leave her bound and exposed in a chair facing the door and if anyone did enter, she would be mortified beyond belief. She doesn't know that I have already forbidden anyone to enter this wing of my ranch when I'm in residence. Nobody will dare go against my wishes and so I take my time and head to the kitchen to gather the supplies I need to torture my prey even further, long into the night.

CHAPTER 24

HOLLY

*W*hat has happened to me? I don't even recognize myself anymore. I've become weak, easily led and taken down a path I should back away from, and fast.

Dexter is seriously depraved. He's doing things to me that are wrong on so many levels, but I'm loving every second of it. Just seeing his looks of lust and promise, makes me feel so powerful knowing I'm the one responsible for placing that look in his eyes.

Seeing how turned on he is makes me even wetter for him and the more disgusting the game, the more I like it and now he's left me bound and exposed, alone in a room after bringing me to the most explosive orgasm of my life. The fact he was fully clothed added to the sordid nature of the 'lesson' and I can't wait to see what else he's got. He may like the weak side of me, but inside I'm on fire.

I want this.

I want him and I want this whole fucked-up situation because emotion has been left at the door while we break every rule that nature crafted over time.

It's all about the sex which suits me just fine because I don't deal well with feelings. Who needs emotion to ruin a perfect orgasm, not me? It's all about a fleeting moment of pleasure with no hang-ups at the end. Dexter isn't seeking love and romance, he's all about sex and the experience and that's absolutely fine with me.

He thinks I'll fall for him, do whatever he wants out of love —for him. Well, he's wrong. I'm in this for my own sexual pleasure and there is nothing wrong with that. When I get bored, I'll end it, simple. I'll use him like he's using me and then I'll take this experience and run with it to a brighter future made possible by what he can give me. Learn the business and enjoy a sexual experience I'm unlikely to ever repeat and who wouldn't be happy with that?

I hear footsteps approaching and pray it's him because I've been on edge ever since he left.

As the door opens, he heads inside and my heart starts beating fast as he approaches.

"Are you comfortable, baby?"

I nod, my mouth dry with anticipation and he says roughly, "Answer me."

"Yes, sir." He nods with satisfaction and sets a tray down on the side. I can't see the contents but I'm mildly curious and then he says softly, "Close your eyes."

My body wakes up in anticipation and a warm glow passes through me as I sense pleasure heading my way and as the cool burn of the ice runs all over my body, I shiver and gasp as it burns against the heat of my pussy. One by one, he places the ice cubes into my opening and it's unbearable. It burns so badly and yet soothes at the same time. Then he places his hot mouth that must be the result of sipping a hot drink and sucks my clit and the mixture of hot and cold makes me tremble and gasp as the different sensations it brings struggle to take control.

As the ice melts inside, the cool river merges with the heat of his tongue as he sucks, licks and causes so much pleasure to build, I'm almost ashamed at how quickly he can bring me to a climax.

As I cry out for the second time, he strokes my breast and just stares and it should freak me right out but somehow feels nice. It's an intimate moment between us, a bond of longing and a closeness that surprises me.

I watch as he stands and heads back toward the tray and removes a white cloth and when he returns, he washes me between the legs and I almost purr with pleasure. The cloth is warm and soft and as he cleans up the evidence of how much he affects me, I'm surprised at how good this feels.

I actually feel a little selfish right now because he has remained clothed throughout and so far the pleasure has been all mine and when he removes the cloth, I say tentatively, "What about you?"

"What about me?" His amused grin makes me a little embarrassed and I say shyly, "Would you like me to..."

"No."

He heads back to the tray and says dismissively, "I get my pleasure from seeing yours. I will give you mine when you have learned the basics."

"Oh, um, ok."

This all feels a little one-sided and I feel like a selfish bitch right now and as he heads back, I squeal in surprise as he liberally smears ice-cream all over my body. Chuckling, he steps back and grins. "The finest dessert. How can I possibly refuse?"

Bending down, he proceeds to lick every trace of it from my body and I gasp and squirm on my seat as I become the most twisted kind of edible treat. My pussy is throbbing with the need for him to fill it and it's almost unbearable as he takes his time, his slurps, sucks and licks making me lose my mind.

I am trembling so much I can't even think straight and once again, as he washes me with the cloth, I start to moan, "Please, sir."

"What, baby, tell me what you want?"

"You, sir, I want you."

To my surprise, he strokes my hair and looks almost lovingly into my eyes, which shocks me a little. Then he nods, a spark in his eyes.

"You have pleased me tonight, you shall get your reward."

He unzips his trousers and I watch with nervous anticipation as he removes his cock and then sheaths it with a condom from his pocket. Still bound and spread out before him, I can't stop staring at the huge length that is even more impressive than I thought what feels like months ago. It looks almost too big and yet I know it fits as it was designed to.

He stands at my opening and if anyone could see this, they would be disgusted at the depraved scene as he stands fully clothed ready to take me in the most basic of ways. As he enters my body, I love the delicious trail of heat that accompanies it and as he slides home, his grunts of pleasure are music to my ears. He isn't gentle either and thrusts inside quickly, roughly and so hard the chair rocks with me tied to it, the leather grazing my wrists and the plastic ties biting into my skin. He drives in so hard I bite my lip as he tears inside my wet heat and I struggle to breathe because this is brutal, rough and so sexy I want more of the same.

He fists my hair and holds my head in place as he pushes in hard and the pleasure builds. On and on he goes until I swear a white light blinds me and I scream so hard he captures it in his mouth and bites down hard. Pleasure mingles with pain and the wave of ecstasy that pumps through my body is the most glorious high and then I almost weep as he pulls back and tears the condom from his cock and using his hand, pumps his seed all over my face and body. Marking me, claiming me and owning me.

For a moment there is silence. There are no words to describe what just happened and I blink as my breathing comes ragged and fast. I feel his mark of ownership running like a sticky trail down my body and, as he pulls back, he rakes my body with a satisfied gaze. "Perfect."

He reaches down and smears his arousal over my breasts and just feeling how dirty this is makes me shiver with desire. What has happened to me indeed because I am getting off on things I would never believe in a million years would excite me so much.

Thankfully, he snaps the ties and unfastens the belt and pulls me from the chair. "Lie on the floor."

He commands me and I obey and as I lie face upwards, he gently cleans my body with care and precision.

As soon as he finishes, he says abruptly, "You may dress now."

Feeling slightly sad about that, I reach for my clothes as he pours us both a coffee from the pot and waves to the couch.

"Drink this."

I do as he says and am grateful for the strong coffee he appears to love so much and feel surprised when he sits in the chair opposite.

After what just happened, this feel so cold and he looks at me with a blank expression and says abruptly, "Tonight we sleep, we have work to do tomorrow and I have decided that for now we sleep in separate rooms."

His words cause me anxiety and I say fearfully, "Have I disappointed you?"

"No." He smiles. "Not at all, but I think we should keep this arrangement strictly professional. Intimacy will be reserved for your lessons and our personal space is ours. It's best this way for both of us because feelings must be kept out of it, do you understand?"

"Yes, sir." For some reason I feel miserable about that because I wanted to lie wrapped in his arms, possibly feel better about my decision, but this just reinforces the fact it's just sex. Cold, yet hot, devastating sex and, after all, isn't that what I want, anyway?

You're a fool, a misguided fool.

That little voice inside my head shouts me down and, in my heart, I know she's right. Can I have sex without emotion? I just did but now I'm not so sure because now he's made it clear what this is, I feel so hurt I want to tuck myself into a ball and cry bitter tears of self-loathing. Why am I not good enough for him, and why does he make me feel like a queen one minute and a whore the next?

As we go our separate ways, I am faced with a long night of recriminations as I go through events in my mind as to what went on here today. Can I really do this? It's so cold it will destroy me in the end. But as I lie in the large comfortable bed, my hands reach for my body imagining they are his. Yes, I'm screwed because I couldn't back out now if I tried.

CHAPTER 25

DEXTER

I changed my mind for a very good reason. When I told Holly she wouldn't sleep with me, it was to keep my own feelings in check. The whole experience in the library shocked me at how much I wanted this woman. I had an urgent need to be close to her at all times and physically ached to hold her and whisper words of love in her ear. That shocked me more than anything.

Through the whole lesson, she never put a foot wrong. She responded better than I dared hope and I couldn't stop. It became a delicious game I wanted to play all night, and I recognized something different. It wasn't what I did; it was *her*.

The woman.

I wanted to please her, to make her fall under my spell because the more I did to her, the more anxious I became that she would leave. So, I made my decision. I'm pulling back, emotionally, because feelings are inconvenient to a man who banned them from his life. I made a promise to myself that I would never love again because it hurts too much when they leave.

I don't go to bed. Instead, I retreat to my den and the past returns as it always does when I'm at my lowest point.

Night time is the worst. It's when my demons come back to haunt me. I can see her as plainly as if she is standing in front of me. Dark unruly hair with aquamarine eyes. Beautiful.

"Come and play, Dexsie."

"I'm busy."

"You're always busy. Come and play, pleeez."

Just her impish grin always made me relent, and I set down my computer game and smiled - she always got her way with me, anyway.

My sister, my best friend. We were so close in age we were almost twins. Joined together by our DNA and alike in so many ways except she was light, I was shade. She was the sun; I was the moon. Opposites that complemented each other and made everything right.

Our childhood was happy, no sibling rivalry or arguments in our case. I loved my sister and always cared for her with an overprotectiveness that annoyed her the older we got.

Boyfriends were vetted, and warned off if there was just a hint they were unworthy. I took my role as her big brother very seriously and it caused many arguments.

Nobody would ever be good enough for my sister and, as it turned out, I was right.

Just thinking about Mario Cordoli makes my skin crawl and the anger resurface. He intrigued her. Flattered her and gave her excitement in a destructive way. The son of a man nobody ever wants to meet on a dark night and a man you upset at your peril.

I went there, anyway.

I tried everything possible to talk her out of it, but her mind was made up. They announced their engagement at Sunday brunch and I stormed from the room in disgust. My parents were powerless to change her mind and powerless against his family. She was a sacrificial lamb to the slaughter and I couldn't bear to stand by and watch her ruin her life in the most destructive of ways.

Back then, I was who I am now. Dexter Prince, King of Media Corp and one of five men who hold the fate of society in our hands. I tried to use my position to dispose of him and used every weapon in my arsenal.

Every piece of dirt I had on him, his family, and everyone connected to them was published in a destructive way. A character assassination of the worst kind that caused so much damage it was like a violent storm hitting and wiping out everything in its path.

My sister was angry and blamed me for everything. Told me she never wanted to see me again and she would marry him or die.

Ironic really, when that's exactly what happened.

As payback for what I did.

We were having our usual Sunday lunch and waiting for Phoebe to arrive. Relations had been strained since I massacred her boyfriend and his family's reputation and it was now at the stage they were under investigation and facing a jail term. She hadn't spoken to any of us in over a month and when we got the text saying she wanted to meet up and discuss things, we were hopeful for a reconciliation. Surely, she could see what a monster she had agreed to marry and knew it was only a matter of time before he ruined her. I had no regrets about what I did because I would do anything to protect her.

We heard the car skidding to a halt outside and I will never forget the look in my parent's eyes as they looked at one another, already sensing something wasn't right.

We raced outside as fast as we could and the only thing there was a crumpled heap on the ground.

I swear my life ended that day as I struggled to make sense of what I saw.

Lying in the gravel was the body of the woman I loved more than anything and the fact she never moved told me everything I needed to know. My mother screamed and the sound of it will live in my memory to my dying day. It was the torturous sound of pain and grief mixed in a life changing cocktail.

My father rushed forward, but I got there first and as I turned her over, my heart broke forever. Her beautiful eyes stared up at me, all the life drained from her soul.

She was dead.

That was the only time I ever saw my father cry. Tears of anguish that caused the lines of grief to live with him to this day. A life lost in the cruelest way and it was all my fault.

As I drink the ever-present glass of whiskey, I feel the burn as I relive for the millionth time the horror of that day.

She had been beaten to death. Bruising to every part of her body, cuts gouged deep into her perfect skin. Two missing ears and her tongue cut out.

Because of what I did.

If I could rewind time, I would in a heartbeat.

If I could undo the wrong, erase the story and do things differently, I would.

As I cradled her lifeless body, my life changed forever and any feeling, any emotion I ever had inside me, left me that day. I don't feel, I *can't* feel, which is why I am locked in a prison of my own making.

The tears still burn as she revisits me at night. Always at night when the air is still and the demons circle. When Hell opens up begging me to jump inside. A tortured soul condemned to eternal damnation because of a rash decision I made with no fear of the consequences.

That is why I have rules set in place to stop something like this ever happening again, because if another person experiences the grief I feel every hour of the day and night, it will all be worthless. The lesson that was thrust at me at a million miles an hour will not go unlearned, and when I saw Holly's story bypass my stringent procedures, I was pissed beyond belief.

Once again, I fill my glass from the dwindling bottle and knock it back to dull the emotion. I won't let it in, but just thinking of Holly lying a few rooms away makes me stop and think. Maybe just one night would help a little. A soft body to cling to, to help me sleep. Protect me from the demons who call. They wouldn't come for me there—surely and so I set the glass down and stagger from the room.

The hallway is silent. The occupants of this ranch fast asleep in their beds. Only the floor light sensors guide me as I stagger with exhaustion fueled by alcohol to find comfort for the night.

As I open the door, I see a heap in the bed illuminated by the moonlight and her steady breathing tells me one of us at least is sleeping.

Removing my clothes, the bed dips as I tuck myself under the sheets and pull her tightly into me. She stiffens as I wake her and I gently kiss her neck and whisper, "It's me, go to sleep."

Her soft sigh settles me and as I stroke her hair, I feel a different kind of emotion grip me. I feel protective of her. She is mine to care for and make sure no harm can come to her.

My slave, my toy, my woman.

I stroke her soft skin and she presses in closer and I kiss her lightly, gently, with care and consideration and whisper, "Go to sleep."

As she sighs with pleasure, the sound settles my heart and I pull her in tight and the demons retreat. Then, for the first time in a long time, I drift off to sleep.

CHAPTER 26

HOLLY

*I*t felt like an exquisite dream.

When the early morning sun touched my skin through the drapes, I felt so happy I could burst. Yesterday was an epiphany. A realization of how good life can be and for the first time in my adult life, I feel no responsibilities weighing me down.

Then I wake and realize I'm alone. Was I dreaming? Surely Dexter was here. He came in the early hours and was so loving, so gentle and caring. It made my heart open and let him in. It felt so good being held as if I was the most precious thing to him. It felt so nice, but when did he leave?

It doesn't make sense and so I shower and dress for the day, starting it off with confusion rather than clarity, as seems to be the case these days.

He's not at breakfast either and Maisy appears deep in her own thoughts this morning and I wonder if anything has happened.

She serves me breakfast and I say tentatively, "Is everything ok?" Part of me is embarrassed in case she heard us in the library. Maybe she's disgusted with me and thinks I'm some kind of whore and wants nothing to do with me.

She looks startled and says sadly, "We lost a calf last night. Jason tried hard to save her but she didn't make it."

"I'm so sorry." I look at her in horror and she sighs heavily. "It doesn't get any easier, you'd think it would."

"Does it happen often?"

"Not so much, but when it does, it reminds you of the fragility of life."

She stirs her coffee and appears to change direction and smiles. "Anyway, tell me about your evening. Have you cracked the man in the suit yet?"

"What do you mean?" I squirm a little and she grins. "Something's changed. I saw it in his eyes this morning. He seemed, well, lighter somehow, like a weight has shifted and excuse me for talking out of turn, but I make his bed and it wasn't slept in."

She winks as I blush and yet before I can think of every excuse under the sun, Dexter arrives like a force of nature and says abruptly, "My office, we have work to do."

She rolls her eyes behind his back and I resist the urge to giggle and as I follow him out, I wonder what mood he'll be in today.

As we walk, he says nothing and just strides to his den like a man on a mission and I almost have to run to catch up.

As soon as we get inside, he says curtly, "That story you've been researching. Do you think you could give it a shot?"

"You mean, write the story—really."

I feel my face light up and for a moment he just stares and then tears his gaze away and sits at his desk. "Yes, see what you can do and then show it to me. I want to test your skills, see what you've learned and only if I pass it, will it print."

I am so stoked I don't know how to begin and for the next six hours I concentrate so hard I miss lunch and only look up when Maisy drops a sandwich and potato chips on the desk with a glass of juice. "Food for the workers."

She smiles and winks as she leaves the room.

I have almost forgotten that Dexter is here because we have both worked silently and methodically for most of the day and as I see the sun burning outside the window, it reminds me that life goes on. Normal life, whatever that is, and the story I am writing like fury will have consequences for the lives it touches.

Dexter's quiet and appears to have his own thoughts dominating his time and as I take a bite of the sandwich, it reminds me not to neglect my routine because I am so hungry, I finish it way too quickly and feel like a pig as he says with amusement, "You obviously needed that."

Laughing nervously, I grin. "Sorry, I kind of forgot about time and didn't realize how hungry I was."

As he takes a bite of his own sandwich, he watches me with a hooded expression and then shocks me by saying, "Do you like it here, Holly?"

For a moment I'm lost for words because it's a strange experience all round and I'm not sure what to think but shrug and smile, "It's different."

"But do you like it?"

For some reason, my answer means a lot to him and so I choose my words carefully.

"I like it—for now."

"Why only now?"

He looks disappointed and I squirm a little. "Well, it's not really normal life, for me, anyway."

"What is?"

He seems interested to hear more, and I shrug. "I work, I eat, I sleep and I clean on weekends. To be honest, work is my life because I want to be the best. I'm not sure where that leaves me now though because when you find my stepbrother everything may change and I'm not sure what that means —for me."

"What do you want your life to be?"

"I told you, I want to work. Be the best journalist I can. Run my own empire I guess, be my own boss and control my own destiny."

"So, you're ambitious."

"Of course."

"What about a family, marriage, babies even, isn't that what most women want?"

I feel my feminist shackles rising and say tightly, "Can't we have it all, sir?"

I raise my eyes and he surprises me by laughing softly and feeling bold, I say, "What about you, what do you want?"

For a moment he looks angry and I regret opening my mouth and then I watch in fascination as a wicked look is thrown my way and he says lazily, "I want you to suck my cock."

"Excuse me."

"You heard."

I'm not sure if he's joking or not, but from the look in his eyes, he means every word and so I stand slightly nervously and walk toward him.

"What if some…"

"Are you questioning me, Holly?"

His eyes flash and I remember his promise of punishment if I displease him and so I shake my head. "No, sir."

"Then on your knees and suck my cock like I told you to."

I sink to my knees and with one eye on the door, I unzip his pants and gasp when his hand pulls down sharply on my hair and he hisses, "Full concentration on me."

The tears build as the pain increases as he pulls harder and I can't remove his cock fast enough and open wide as he thrusts into my mouth. Using my own head to anchor me down, he thrusts in and out of my mouth roughly, without care, and for once this isn't a pleasurable experience because he is using me and treating me like a piece of disposable trash. As he comes, I feel the salty spunk coat my mouth, throat and tongue and I gag a little and he hisses, "Swallow every drop."

The tears fall as he increases the pressure on my head, and I wonder why he changed so quickly. As soon as I'm done, he pushes me away and growls, "Back to work."

For a moment, I'm stunned. What just happened? He changed like a light switch from easy-going to a monster. As I retreat back to my work, I struggle to find a reason for it, replaying our conversation over and over in my mind, and yet there's nothing. Is he mad, should I be freaking the hell out right now because what he just did was cruel and I feel cheap, used and dirty?

There's a large part of me that will never be ok with what just happened, so I grab hold of that and run with it and say loudly, "May I have a word, sir."

"What is it?"

He seems irritable and I swallow any nerves I have and say tightly, "I want an explanation."

"I owe you nothing."

Feeling the fury rising, I snap. "Wrong. You can't treat me like I'm nothing. Like I have no feelings, no rights and no right to respect. You won't even tell me why you just degraded me; don't I have a right to know?"

"You think I degraded you, I told you what was involved."

I feel my eyes flash as I approach his desk and stare him right in the eye as I hiss, "You never mentioned I would feel like this. How dare you make me feel worthless, disposable and if my feelings don't count? Well, you can stick your apprentice-ship up your..."

"ENOUGH!"

His voice is loud and angry and shocks me into silence as he stands and the fire blazing from his eyes scares me—a lot.

I almost think he's going to strike me when he raises his hand and I flinch and watch as his eyes darken and he says huskily, "Take a seat, Holly and I will explain."

Hating myself for being so weak, I sink into the chair opposite him and he says darkly, "I didn't like our conversation."

"What do you mean?"

I am genuinely confused, which once again reinforces my realization that I'm facing a madman.

"You spoke about a life outside of this one. It's what you hope for your future, telling me you are unhappy with our —situation."

"But…"

He holds up his hand. "I told you if you displeased me, angered me, there would be consequences. You made me doubt my offer to teach you, to mentor you and show you a better way."

"I'm sorry, sir, but I still don't understand."

He sighs and looks a little lost, which makes me worry for him and he says in a whisper, "I want you to stay. To see this through and learn. I want to give you everything you want, Holly, but I want it to be on my terms. Bringing you here was a big risk, asking you to fulfill the role you're in was a very big risk and I thought you understood. You need to trust me and I need to control you, that's how this works. If you can't, then there's no point, you will have to go."

"Go."

"Suddenly, I'm fearful of what I'd wished for so desperately a few days ago. Now the thought of leaving him is strangely disturbing and I wonder if I've been drawn into the madness and my head has been screwed as well as my body.

"Yes. You remain here under my terms or not at all, it's your choice."

I watch in shock as he stands and says roughly, "I'm going out. Stay here and finish the job you started, if you can lower yourself, that is."

Before I can even breathe, he is gone and as the key turns in the lock, I am once again a prisoner and feel as if I'm right back where I started.

CHAPTER 27

DEXTER

I need air and fast.

I'm not sure what happened back there, but when she said she wanted to carry on with her dream—before this—before *me*, it made me *feel*. I don't want to feel. I don't want to form attachments and if she decides to go, where will that leave me?

I know I'm a selfish bastard; I want it all and on my terms only. It's ridiculous to expect her to give up her dreams—her future to become my fuck toy, and I know I'm being unreasonable. But emotion hit me and I didn't like it.

I need to reassess this whole situation before it destroys me and so I head outside in search of Jason.

I find him at the stables and as I see him saddling up his horse, I say evenly, "Hey, do you fancy some company?"

"Sure, it's been a long time, I'll get your horse."

He hands the reins to me of Midnight, his own stallion and while I wait, I stroke the mane of the impressive horse who responds favorably to my touch. He nuzzles my hand and I wish I had something to give him, cursing myself for not bringing the usual mints he loves.

Jason doesn't take long and leads out my own stallion, Saracen, who seems pleased to see me even though it's been a few months since my last visit.

"Horses are loyal, they never forget." He chucks me a cowboy hat and I smile my thanks.

Jason looks at me with a considered expression "How are things?"

We haul ourselves into the saddle and Jason leads off at a slow walk, giving us time to catch up.

"Could be better."

"Do you wanna talk about it?"

"Probably best not to."

He nods and points to the horizon.

"Rains heading our way and not before time. The grass is fading and the herd hungry."

Thinking of the hot summer we've had so far, I share his concern. Although we have enough food for the animals, it's not the same as letting them graze freely.

I'm surprised when he says in his lazy drawl, "You know, animals are a lot like our women."

"This I've got to hear."

I roll my eyes as he chuckles. "Tend them well, keep them happy and they reward you with loyalty."

"So, you treat Maisy like Midnight, I'm sure she's super happy about that."

Jason laughs, his deep, lazy laugh that always relaxes me.

"Maisy knows how it works. She cares for me, and I care for her. We only want the best and if one is happy, so is the other."

"But what if she leaves, what then? It would have all been for nothing and you would be broken."

He falls silent and I know I'm right. Then he says with a slow chuckle, "Then you don't wanna go giving them a reason to leave."

He kicks his horse to a canter and as I chase after him, I

love the exhilaration this always gives me. Riding fast through my property with not another building in sight. My own paradise, a land of my own that I have full control over. As I see the barren fields that we pass and see the devastation the drought has caused, it strikes me that control is a fragile thing. Do we really have full control—ever? Nature is the decider and if she decides to strike, there's no escaping your fate.

Jason pulls up and I catch my breath and we share a grin. Most of the time, I envy Jason and Maisy. They have a good, happy life with no worries. They love living off the land and the generous pay check I deal out but I wouldn't have it any other way. They have a home here for life and it's more their home than mine, anyway. One day they will have a family and bring them up here and I will love every second of it. I can watch from afar and share in their lives with none of the responsibility because I don't want any. I don't deserve it.

As we lean on our horses looking out on the sun setting on the horizon, I think of Holly working away, locked in her prison. She would love to see this and I feel ashamed of myself. Jason's right. What reason outside sex have I given her to make her want to stay? She needs to be free to a point, to enjoy what I can give her in every way. Not what I think she wants, but what makes her happy.

Feeling like a fool, I check myself because, in giving Holly what she wants, I lay myself open to emotion and I'm not prepared for that. However, as Saracen neighs and stamps the ground, I reach out and pat his mane. "There, there boy, one minute more."

Jason laughs. "He's impatient to please you. Nothing compares to a ride from his master, he only fully opens up to you."

Thinking about the way I indulge my horse makes me happy. He has everything he needs and my undivided attention when I'm here. I treat him well and he rewards me with devotion. Do I love my horse, you bet I do and yet how is that the same? He's an animal. They have different expectations?

Jason is watching me, and I know he's concerned. Normally when I'm here, I spend most of my time with the couple I prefer above anyone else, except for Sam, who is like a brother to me.

But Holly, there's something different about her I just can't put my finger on and as we turn the heads of our horses and give them free rein, I'm in a different mind when I return than when I left.

I WASTE no time and set off to find her and as I turn the key in the lock, I feel ashamed that I felt the need to keep her imprisoned. The signals I am sending out are mixed and I need to remedy that before we can continue.

She looks up as I enter and I note the dark shadows under her eyes and the weary look she throws my way. Realizing how badly she needs some fresh air, I feel bad that I have enjoyed something she is desperate to receive.

Crouching down beside her, I look at the article she has been working on and say softly, "How's it going?"

"I'm just finishing off."

She suppresses a yawn and I take her hand and pull her up and into my chest, and then leaning down I whisper, "I'm sorry."

She says nothing but stiffens a little, indicating her surprise and I sigh, stroking her hair much like I just did to Saracen.

"You don't deserve this treatment. I'm playing hot and cold with your emotions and that's not ok."

She still says nothing and I feel like an inconsiderate bastard and hate how I must look in her eyes, so kissing the top of her head lightly, I whisper, "Enough work for one day. Go and shower and change for dinner. I need to look after you."

She pulls back and looks confused, and I kiss her gently on the lips. "Let me make it up to you."

I hate that she's even considering her options right now because I see the doubt in her eyes and know she must have been doing some thinking herself in my absence and yet she just nods and says coolly. "Ok, I owe you that at least."

I hate this wall that has formed between us and know it's there because I built it and so as I watch her go, I decide to make things right for her. She needs to feel comfortable around me, enjoy the time we spend together because even though nothing has really changed and I still don't want emotion, I do want *her* and I will do whatever's necessary to keep her.

CHAPTER 28

HOLLY

Obviously, Dexter did a lot of thinking when he was gone because he returned a very different person to the one who left. As I shower and change, I think about my situation and know I'm screwed before he even 'makes it up to me.'

I want him.

I desire him and I want the opportunity he can give me, but I'm not sure I want the whole control thing. In my mind, trust needs to come before control and right now, I trust him as much as any woman kidnapped against her will and thrown into prison.

Sighing, I set about getting ready and change into an emerald green dress that sits just above my knee. This one disguises my curves and I do so for a reason, because I want Dexter to look at Holly, not the body he so obviously craves. I'm sick of being his fuck toy, although I can think of nothing else when he's around. I'm even ashamed to admit that I loved the rough treatment earlier, which shows I need to get the hell out of here and fast. He can't think that I'm ok with that because then he will have a license to do whatever he likes—to me and I need to put a stop to it if I am ever going to leave with my insanity intact.

My hair is brushed until it shines and hangs naturally, dusting the small of my back and I make up my eyes to match my mood, dark and sexy because one thing's for sure, I relish anything he can give me in that department. Dexter Prince is like sex cocaine. One sniff and you're addicted and desperate for more. I want to overdose on his particular drug and I'm ashamed, like any addict, how weak I am when it comes to it. But he can be so cruel and I'm not ok with that, so tonight we need to draw some lines that can't be crossed and I need to get into the part of my head that conducts business above everything else.

To my surprise, when I enter the kitchen, Maisy looks up and smiles. "Hey, honey, you look gorgeous. I love that color on you."

"Thanks, Maisy." I always love seeing the pretty housekeeper who looks like bubble gum and ponies all rolled into one sexy package. Her husband is the stuff of cowboy dreams and any children they produce will win the genetic lottery.

She quickly says, "Dexter asked that you meet him in the library."

My heart sinks. Great, the sex room. How can I possibly negotiate with him surrounded by memories of how amazing I felt when I was last in there?

Nodding, I head that way, feeling nervous and yet full of anticipation. To be honest, one crook from his finger and I would strip in seconds because I could do with losing myself in an orgasm or two right now. Maybe we can talk later because I kind of love the escape sex with him gives me. It makes me think of nothing but pleasure and after the past week living with the anxieties I have, any release from that is a welcome one.

When I push open the door, I'm surprised to see the room

bathed in candlelight and the man himself standing by the fire-place looking so hot he should be burning in the grate. Black trousers and a white shirt, undone enough to show his extremely masculine chest, act like the lure of the sirens as I step inside. His dark, flashing eyes watch me approach and strip me of every ounce of resistance I brought with me. The way he even looks at me makes me feel as if I've committed a sin because that look means business and I'm ready to sign the contract.

Is Dexter Prince the devil in a not so clever disguise and am I being tested because if so, I'm about to fail big time because my mouth is watering and it's not for the food?

"Holly, you look beautiful."

Feeling myself blush like a fucking idiot, I smile softly, "Thank you, um, well, you too."

I sound like a cheerleader crushing over the quarterback, and he smiles, telling me he knows exactly how I'm feeling right now.

Holding out his hand, he says warmly, "Come and sit down. I have some champagne on ice, a vintage I'm sure you will love."

Hell, any champagne is a treat to me, even the bargain one they sell in Publix is more than my budget allows and so I smile and take the seat opposite him and grab the glass with eager fingers, as he says pleasantly, "We should toast our arrange-ment but I feel that's a little premature. I expect you need more details to make your final decision."

He's not wrong about that, but one word strikes me more than most.

"You say final, what does that mean?"

He sits before me and just the way he casually dangles the glass between his legs has me imagining all sorts of dirty twisted thoughts and he says casually, "I need to give you a better reason to stay."

Looking up, I note the determination in his eyes and say with surprise, "Stay. For how long?"

"That's up to you."

"Is it, it doesn't feel that way?"

I take a large gulp of the cool, calming liquid and love how decadent I feel right now as I sip champagne with the master.

"I'm aware I've fucked up the earliest part of your training and want to reassure you that it won't happen again. I know you have no reason to believe me, but I want this to work."

Feeling a little bold, I say roughly, "You say arrangement, I'm still not sure what that is exactly."

"My apprentice during the day and my partner at night. Submissive, if you want a label for it."

I'm still confused. "But how will that work? It sounds to me as if you want me around 24/7. Surely, we would hate each other inside a week. Also, how would that look? People would think I was screwing the boss to get ahead and they would be right. I can't do both, surely."

He looks angry and I think I've spoken out of turn as he sighs and shakes his head. "I make my own rules and the staff can suck it up."

"No." I feel my eyes flash with an energy that surprises me as he raises his eyes. "No?"

"I want to earn people's respect. If I'm to do this, nobody must know you are doing me any favors."

He falls silent and I can tell he's wrestling with something and for some reason, I feel weary. Just talking about this like it's some form of contract is not sitting well with me. He wants to control every part of me and as much as I like the thought of being with him, the terms suck because he just wants me for sex and the job is the golden carrot designed to trap me.

I'm almost crying when I shake my head and say sadly, "I can't agree to something I feel uncomfortable with, as much as I desire the opportunity. Right now, I have nothing—you've seen to that and in your eyes am in the perfect place to agree to everything you say. You hold all the cards and I have nothing; how can I sacrifice my principles under those terms?"

I look up and smile regretfully. "I do want you, sir. For the most part, I'm enjoying this experience but it's not enough. If I'm honest, I'm a little afraid of you. You turn in a split second and the way you made me feel earlier, well, it made me feel —disposable."

He nods and my heart sinks as I sense him retreating and know I've just signed my exit strategy.

Taking another slug of my drink, I place it on the side and say regretfully, "Maybe we should keep things strictly professional from now on and when I'm allowed to leave, I'll look for another job."

"Holly."

His deep voice sounds commanding and yet wrapped in softness, and I look at him nervously.

"I want you to trust me, understand me even, and so I need to tell you something that may shock you. I'm not sure if I can even complete the sentences but I'm going to try—because I value what we could have."

This is so unexpected and I stare at him in surprise and yet hang onto his every word because I so need to hear whatever he has to say.

He appears a little lost for words and that's so unlike him and as the tortured expression reflects back at me, I hitch my breath as I wait for what he thinks will change everything.

"I can't love. I can't allow myself that luxury because of something that happened in my past."

He exhales sharply and I prepare myself for the old story of an unrequited love or something, a betrayal perhaps, but nothing prepares me for the story he tells me through faltering speech and fractured sentences. There is no emotion as he tells me the circumstances surrounding his sister's death and the dead way he speaks make my heart break. He delivers the shocking tale as if he's talking about someone else proving to me that Dexter Prince is fifty shades of fucked up.

As he breaks off, he looks me directly in the eye and says dully, "Any questions?"

For a moment I can't form words because the horror of his past deserves better comment than any I can think of and I say softly, "I'm sorry,"

He nods. "Thank you."

I feel a little confused and wonder if I should say anything because I heard a very different story to this one and he says calmly, "Spit it out, Holly."

"I'm sorry."

"Yes, you already said that. Tell me what you're thinking."

"I'm sorry…" He raises his eyes and I say quickly, "It's just that I read your sister died from a mystery illness. I read none of what you've told me. The mafia connection. I don't even recall a trial, or anything about the incident in the news. How can that be because surely this would have been running in the news for months, if not years?"

He nods and my breath hitches when he stares at me with so much power in his eyes, I am instantly speechless. Dexter Prince is most definitely the devil because just that one look alone, tells me that he can indeed do anything he wants, even re-write history.

CHAPTER 29

DEXTER

I have trusted Holly in order to gain her trust and it's a bitter pill to swallow. Telling her my most private story is something I have never told anyone but Ryder in my life. My staff know parts of it – the parts I want them to know but Holly, she deserves the full story because I am putting my heart on the line to gain her trust. In doing so, I am expecting hers in return and if any part of this story gets out, I will know where it came from.

But she wants more, she's not fooled and now I must open up another part of my soul to her which doesn't make sense to me. Why am I trusting this woman with my darkest secret – for sex? For control, to keep her to break her. I don't know what the hell I'm thinking right now and am definitely not in the right frame of mind to discuss my organization. She can't know about that, so I fabricate the truth a little and just say firmly, "I told you, I *am* the news and I make it what I want it to be to suit my purposes. You should know that first hand."

She still looks confused and I stare her straight in the eye and say with determination. "I want you to trust me, to know that I have your best interests at heart and in opening up to you, I want you to see why I'm this way. How can I ever lead a normal life as much as I would love nothing more? I surround myself with a select group of people who I trust with my life. I employ them which means I control them to a point. Do they seem unhappy to you, do I treat them well and can they leave when they want to? Yes, to all of the above and what I'm offering you is on the same terms. I can give you the world, Holly - everything you want but it has to be on my terms. We can negotiate the details to suit but you have to know that I want you in my life but it must be this way."

She appears to think about my words and as I sip the cool champagne, I see a life stretching out before me that seems like an impossible dream. Can I have it all, can we negotiate everything I want into this contract? Possibly, but will it ever be enough?

"Tell me what you're thinking."

I need to know and she says sadly, "What if I want it all, sir? What if I want the dream?"

"What is your dream?"

"I want to be happy."

"And."

"To be loved, to be free and to be able to live my life with someone who loves me back. Like Maisy and Jason. I want that. Equals and in love, not a business deal with the words written with my soul."

Thinking of my next sentence extremely carefully, I set down my glass and lean forward, staring her in the eyes.

"Don't we all want that, Holly? Don't you think I want that too? To be free of the past and at peace. Telling you my darkest secret was a huge step for me and one I never thought would ever be heard. When I left you earlier, I hated what happened. The thought of you leaving me and my reaction to that. That told me I need to practise what I preach and earn your trust, not demand it. I was asking something of you I wasn't prepared to reciprocate and telling you about Phoebe is the hardest thing I have ever done. Maybe over time the edges will soften and fade but it won't happen if I'm alone. I can't promise you more than what I have but surely it's a start. I want this to work because when I found you, something checked a box in my head and it felt right. Fucked-up I know but it feels to me as if you are meant to be here. I want to show you my world and I want to be a part of yours but I'm a dominant, Holly and I can't change that. It's how I cope with life. I need to control it because when I lost control, the most important person in my life died. If you choose to leave, I won't stop you. This has to be your choice but it has to be on my terms, negotiable, of course."

The look on her face fills me with a mixture of fear and excitement because this could go either way because it's obvious she's tempted. Just the yearning in her eyes and the wild look in them tells me she is so perfect for me. Yet she's conflicted because she's a strong woman and giving control to me is against everything she stands for, which is what excites me the most. I like to break a stallion and she is no different. It's all about control with me and yet sitting behind that is a deep need to be loved and to love in my own sick and twisted way.

She shakes her head sadly and says a little hesitantly, "I'm sorry to say this, sir but from where I'm sitting, I see your past differently."

I stare at her long and hard as she says sadly, "It was that act of control that meant you lost it. We don't always have that power, no matter how much we want to, because people have their own minds; their own plan of action and that is what's so sad about your whole situation. I'm not saying you were wrong to do what you did, hell, I would have done the same. You weren't to know what you were dealing with so don't blame yourself for something you could never have controlled and in trying to wrap up your life in the same way, it will only end badly."

I'm hating every word out of her mouth right now because she is throwing everything back in my face and deservedly so.

"Don't you think I know that, Holly." I sigh heavily.

"That I caused it and my actions signed my sister's death warrant. There's not a day that goes by when I don't regret what I did, wished I'd approached things differently, anything but what happened. It's my cross to bear and it will never leave me, so I have to control that side of me that acts impulsively and with actions clouded by emotion. Do you understand?"

"Yes."

Her voice sounds husky and doesn't fit the response I was expecting and I look up in surprise.

"Yes what, Holly?"

I'm actually shocked when she sets her glass down and stands and walks toward me slowly and deliberately.

Kneeling before me, she takes my own glass and sets it on the side and takes my hands and then holding them to her heart she says breathlessly, "Yes, I'll agree to your terms on one condition."

"Which is?"

I hold my breath as I wait for the deal breaker and she whispers, "You never make me feel like I'm beneath you. If we do this, we do it as equals and I will give it my best shot."

"No emotion."

I hate myself for how dead my voice sounds and she smiles sadly. "If that's what makes you happy, sir, no emotion but just for the record, I think you feel a lot of emotion that you choose to ignore. Maybe you don't even realize it but you have a lot to give. Not materially speaking but emotionally. So, if I have to feel enough for the both of us, I will. But the minute you break my rule and make me feel cheap and used, I walk away. Understood?"

Tipping her beautiful face toward me, I smile into her gorgeous eyes. "Understood."

For some reason my heart feels light and as if a weight has shifted and as I pull her up and onto my lap, I kiss Holly Bryant with a soft passion that feels good. Cementing a depraved deal that could ruin us both but somehow seems the right thing to do. Trust and control go hand in hand in my book and I won't break her trust in me but I intend on controlling the hell out of this woman and she is soon going to learn how amazing that can be.

CHAPTER 30

HOLLY

*Y*ou're a fool. As soon as the words left my lips, I knew it was always going to be yes. The feminist inside me, the strong woman who takes no shit and has ambition tattooed on her soul, mocks me as I fold under the most exquisite pressure.

I want him. The man who just opened up like a beautiful, impressive, rare breed of plant and showed me the beauty inside. He trusted me with something that must have been unbearable to witness and then live with forever more. To tell someone even part of that story would be difficult, but just seeing the dead expression on his face when he relayed it made my heart break and my head understand. Can I help? Possibly not, but I want to. I want to bring some light to his world, to help him heal and yet I'm under no illusions it will be recip-rocated.

Dexter wants to control me. To be his sex toy and to be his partner in life that he gets to mold into his idea of the perfect woman. No emotion, no shit because that man has emotion written in war paint on his soul. He is a challenge, a definite challenge, but I'm always up for those and as I sit cradled in his arms, I am forgiven everything because this almost feels normal.

Dinner tonight is a more intimate affair. We talk, we laugh and, to anyone watching, we have known each other for years. Tonight, everything that happened before is paused to resume at a later date, because tonight, we are normal.

"So, baby, tell me how you came to work for Media Corp?"

I can tell he is genuinely interested, and I smile. "I've always been ambitious; I suppose it comes with the territory of not having much as a child. The only thing I was good at was writing, and I had a thirst for knowledge that journalism seemed to quench. My father is in the military but you already know that."

He laughs softly and I roll my eyes. "In fact, you probably know everything about me already. I'm guessing you do your homework, Mr. Prince, and could tell me my favorite color, best day ever and the current state of my bank account."

"Maybe, then again, there's an important part of you I'm struggling with."

"I think you've discovered every part of me, sir."

I flutter my eyelashes and he raises his glass in a salute, "And what an enjoyable voyage of discovery it was."

Suddenly, he looks more serious. "No, it's your mind I have no control over and that scares me because I don't know what you're thinking. Do you play poker, Holly?"

"No, why?"

"Because you'd be a natural. You give nothing away, which is a good trait to have when you're learning about people's lives and shocking news first-hand. You don't let your emotions show, I like that."

"Says the man who won't allow emotion into his life. I kind of expected you would."

"Touché."

Once again, he raises his glass and I smile.

"This is nice."

"It is."

"It almost feels as if this is our first real conversation and it's been well over a week since you ruined my life and made me your prisoner. Goodness, how time flies."

He laughs softly and I love how that makes him look. More relaxed, the stress lines banished and a more carefree dictator than the dominant, angry, powerful one I have come to expect.

Leaning on the table, I say with interest, "This place, have you had it long?"

"A while, possibly seven years, but it could be eight."

"Do you come here often?"

I wink and he shakes his head. "Not as much as I'd like, which reminds me, I have an interesting activity planned for us tonight."

Now I'm almost squirming because I wondered when he'd bring it back to the reason he wants me here. In fact, I feel a little sad about that because conversation counts for a lot when you're getting to know one another. Sex is great, more than great, but I'm learning a lot about him tonight and I'm starting to like the man behind the monster.

Almost as if he can read minds, he says almost sadly, "Tonight is necessary to show you who I really am. I want you to be comfortable around me. I want you to be able to ask me anything and not be afraid I'll bite your head off. I may be the one in charge but I am human after all and this—arrangement can work well for us both."

"How do you imagine it working, I'm curious?"

For the first time, I realize he hasn't colored in the details and he smiles.

"Maybe we should head to the den. I have it all waiting."

Just like that, the moment of intimacy is gone, and it reverts back to a business transaction. Hiding my disappointment about that, I say brightly, "Of course, can I bring my champagne, I think I've developed quite a taste for it."

Reaching out, he grabs the bottle and winks. "Good idea, it will come in handy."

As we walk from the room, I wonder what he's going to raise a toast to because if there's anything waiting that I don't like, I'm calling time on this. Period.

CHAPTER 31

DEXTER

*J*t's time to get down to business and just being in the same room as her was temptation at its finest. I feel extremely pleased with how this has all worked out. For me. Yes, Holly appears happy with how things are. I'm more than happy and I can actually see this working.

Holly will become my partner, for want of a better word, and I will treat her better than she would ever dare imagine in return for her loyalty, trust, and control over her.

Perfect.

As we head into the room, I say evenly, "Take a seat. I have the terms and conditions all ready to go."

"Are you serious?" She seems a little shocked and I shrug. "Of course, I'm a businessman, it's what we do and before you get offended by that, it's for your benefit, not mine."

I can tell she's a little hurt, but I shrug it aside. She needs to know the rules before we begin, and this is the best possible time for that.

As I pull the document from the folder on my desk, I slide it across in her general direction.

"You can see it all laid out in black and white. A contract of employment for your apprenticeship with Media Corp."

She seems to relax a little and looks a little more interested as she glances at the paragraphs neatly printed for her eyes only.

I lean back and wait for her to read the document and know there is nothing in it that would cause concern. I have been overly generous, given her exactly what she wants and the sparkle in her eyes as she raises them to mine, tells me she's more than happy about that.

"It's too much." I love the happiness in her eyes right now, knowing that I put it there, and it makes me feel quite good for once. I like giving her things, making her happy because it completely transforms her. She is stunning, but now she's like a goddess and my cock stirs at the thought of the next contract she will receive tonight.

Handing her a pen, I nod toward the bottom line.

"If you sign it, you're employed immediately."

Her fingers grip the pen and as she hovers over the line, I would be almost disappointed if she didn't ask her next question.

"Is this everything, the only, um, contract I need to sign?"

"No, Holly, there's one more."

"And if I only want to sign one, what happens then?"

"Nothing. You still become my apprentice. I told you I'm a man of my word. You gave me the information I needed, and this is your reward, but it doesn't come without a lot of hard work attached. I don't go easy on my staff, especially ones I work so closely with."

She seems so happy it makes me smile, which is rare indeed, and as she signs her name with a flourish, I feel a certain pride in what I just did. I have cemented her future and given her the dream.

Now it's my turn.

Grabbing the second folder, I hope to God she signs this one because this is the one that interests me the most. *My* dream.

As I slide it across the desk, her jaw drops as she reads the fine print and the nervous way she taps her finger on the desk and looks a little hot is almost unbearable to watch. I am so turned on right now I could lose the control I pride myself on and she swallows—hard.

"Is this a joke?"

"Am I laughing?"

"But it's so…"

"So, what?"

"Cold."

"It only looks that way, Holly. You are reading it in black and white, but we both know there's shade involved. What particular point don't you like?"

"It well…" She clears her throat and tries to mirror my business-like approach.

"I will always be ready for you whenever you ask, regardless of how I feel."

"Yes."

"What if I'm sick?"

"I will be the judge of that."

Shaking her head, she says, "If I displease you, you reserve the right to punish me. What the hell does that mean?"

"Don't displease me and you will never find out."

"Excuse me but I need to know, now, actually."

She looks a little angry, which excites me, and I say darkly, "If I catch you flirting, if I don't have your full attention and if you talk back to me in public, those kinds of things."

"Then you will…" She looks a little fearful and I shrug.

"Spanking mainly. I may tether you to my bed, deprive you of orgasm, confiscate your possessions, that kind of thing."

"For talking to another guy—are you serious?"

She sounds incredulous, and I shrug. "Not talking, Holly, flirting, there's a big difference."

"But what if they flirt with me, how can I change that?"

"It's how you deal with it that counts. Anyway, why are you bothered about the punishments, I can't imagine ever having to chastise you because you haven't upset me so far, have you?"

Her breathing is slightly irregular, and she says huskily, "Have you forgotten when you attacked me for talking back to you because I haven't?"

She takes her pen and draws a line through the paragraph and says icily, "Clause number seven, denied."

Leaning back, I smirk. "You may decide to change your mind on that."

"Why would I?" She looks utterly horrified and I lean forward and fix her with my darkest look and whisper, "Because we both know you loved every second of it."

I love how she squirms on her seat and just the flush in her cheeks tells me I am right and she quickly looks down and laughs softly, "I must call you sir in the office and the bedroom but when we are in casual company, I may call you Dexter. Wow, I'm honored."

She shakes her head and I shrug. "I thought that was fair."

The amusement in her eyes makes me happier and I know she will sign. There may be a few more lines through it, but I expected that. She will learn, though. Holly hates to think she's the perfect submissive, but she is. I knew that the second she walked toward me in Media Corp, hating every minute of the humiliation she was suffering, yet she did it anyway against every screaming bone in her body.

By the time she finishes, there are several lines slashed through the page and I'm a little disappointed to see she's not a fan of the whip, flogger, or bondage. She'll learn and I resign myself to a longer time teaching her how much plea- sure they give but am impatient to get things started, so as soon as she scrawls her signature on the dotted line, I pounce.

"You're mine now, in every way possible."

She looks up at me shyly as I stand towering over her and says softly, "It appears so."

Pulling her from the chair, I grind my lips to hers in a mad frenzy because I have never felt as powerful as the moment she signed her life away to me.

She moans against my mouth and it would be so easy to fuck her all night but tonight is all about setting the tone of our relationship, so I stand back and say darkly, "I want you to strip for me."

Her heightened color sends a surge of lust to my already crazed cock and she nods and reaches for her zipper and pulls it down in one swift move. My breath hitches when I see what I've just acquired and as my eyes feast on her body, I growl, "All of it."

Slowly and sensuously, she removes every delicious strip of silk lingerie and the silence in the room is only interrupted by the clock ticking on the wall. I love that she has lost her nerves because she hasn't even looked at the door once, telling me she's ready.

"Kneel." My voice is husky, and she kneels gracefully down before me, naked and proud and every wish I ever had is granted as she falls at my feet. I know she's enjoying this and isn't playing the victim here because this is a delicious game we both appear to want to play.

CHAPTER 32

HOLLY

I hate that I'm loving every minute of this.

I hate that I just signed my life away for every dream I ever had. In return, I have sacrificed my soul because who the fuck agrees to be a rich man's plaything for a job offer?

I do, because I'm screwed, fucked up and sliding down the water slide to hell in a hand basket.

I don't care. The words that swam before my eyes on that page excited me more than repelled me and, knowing that I can leave at any time, gave me a freedom I never thought he'd agree to. Dexter has surprised me—a lot. He wants this arrangement and I kind of understand why. Hearing his story was heartbreaking and I'm not deluded enough to think I can make him fall in love with me and get the fairy tale, but we can certainly have fun together and maybe this could work.

Nothing in that contract made me feel cheap or beneath him. He was right; it was for my benefit because he doesn't get anywhere near as much as he's offering me. Becoming his sex toy is the creamer on top of the coffee because who wouldn't want a man like him in their bed?

I really hit the jackpot here, except for one thing. I sacrificed my stepbrother and haven't even asked after him.

As he towers above me, I feel the sexual energy in the room that pushes out the questions I need to ask and his deep voice melts me inside as he says huskily, "Lie with your elbows on the desk, face down and push your ass into the air.

I feel so turned on right now because I'm guessing he's going to fuck me against the contract that lies like a red flag before me as I prepare to be lit into flames.

However, the man is more depraved than I thought because I feel the cool, cold, hard, glass of the champagne bottle held against my pussy and I gasp as he inches it a little inside, whispering, "Do you like that, baby?"

It feels cool and a little unpleasant but so wicked I gasp with desire, "Yes."

Carefully, he pushes it in further and flicks my clit with his fingers, and I shudder as he gently bites my neck. So many feelings are rushing through me right now and I tremble as the bottle enters my body, feeling so wrong and yet so intoxicating at the same time. As he plays with my clit and stimulates my senses, I feel the orgasm almost crashing into me as I try to push it away. His low chuckle accompanies me on the ride down and, as I shiver in ecstasy, he pulls me around to face him and holds the dripping bottle to my lips. "Drink the champagne and taste your own blend."

As the bottle enters my mouth, I love the wicked gleam in his lust-filled eyes as I suck on the bottle and the champagne spills down my breasts as he tips it further and faster down my throat.

I groan as he laps at my chest as he tastes the fine wine and my head rolls back as I love every sordid minute of it. Then his fingers pump inside me, searching for yet another orgasm and it's almost unbearable until he hits the spot that makes me scream his name.

As I come hard on his fingers for the second time in a matter of minutes, I love everything about that contract and congratulate myself on winning the sex jackpot. "No regrets?" he whispers in my ear, and I shake my head like a besotted fool.

"No regrets." As he kisses my lips, I hope those words don't come back to bite me because surely, I am now living the dream.

IT'S ONLY when I wake in my own bed with a cold empty space beside me that I realize what I signed up for last night. I feel like a well-used toy as I feel the burn between my legs. Not from him, though. I have yet to receive that particular pleasure because once again, Dexter stripped me bare and fucked me raw but didn't come inside me. The tears burn as I feel the loss of that. It's the part of him I crave the most, his release. He always holds back, though. He gets to a point and then retreats, his seed coating me everywhere else but inside my pulsating pussy.

I want to feel that bond, the closeness that two people enjoy as they collapse against one another after mind-blowing sex. But it's all a game to him. A delicious game of control that he excels at winning.

I spent the night alone again. We parted at the door and this time he didn't pay me a visit in the deepest part of the night. I sleep alone, that was paragraph 12B, and it mocks me as like a fool. I thought it was just print on paper. He meant it, though. What happened the other night was a one off, he told me. A moment of madness he would make sure was not repeated.

That makes me feel like shit and I wonder how far I will let him make me fall before I reach out to stop myself from hitting the deck.

Breakfast feels a little different today. An understanding has been reached and there's a lightness to the atmosphere that wasn't there before. Dexter appears more relaxed and I wonder if it's a good time to raise the subject of my stepbrother. However, the man who brought me from the cold prison outside has joined us today and it feels a little embarrassing. I know this is Sam, his bodyguard slash assistant, and the curious look he gives me makes me squirm a little with embarrassment. In fact, it's a full house this morning because Maisy and Jason are also here and from the knowing looks the three of Dexter's friends share between them, tells me they know exactly how our relationship has moved on.

Dexter is oblivious and just gazes broodingly at his phone and it's left to Maisy to make small talk until Dexter looks at Sam.

"We need to talk."

For some reason, something on his phone is causing him concern and Sam just nods with a blank expression and they leave the room almost immediately.

Maisy sighs and smiles at Jason. "So, honey, what's the plan for today?"

"Moving the herd. We're running out of grazing pasture and need to move them on so we can water and restore the one they're in."

"It will rain soon; I just know it."

She smiles at him reassuringly. "The weather channel said it could rain, there's a small chance."

He smiles at her as if she just promised him the world and it feels a little uncomfortable witnessing a moment between two people who are so obviously crazy about one another. They are a striking couple who are so good and kind I wonder what they would think of my own arrangement. I'm pretty certain they would be shocked and I feel a little ashamed of that.

Maisy doesn't seem the kind of woman to settle for anything less than the fairy tale, and she certainly got that because Jason is every red-blooded woman's cowboy fantasy. Tanned skin, startling blue eyes and dark tousled hair, that is cropped close with a body that is a fine result of working outdoors, from his strong abs and biceps that could wrestle a bear. Maisy is a pretty wholesome girl with blonde curls and baby blue eyes with a body that would be the envy of most women. I always wanted to be the textbook willowy blonde but Maisy has changed my mind on that because her curves are far more desirable from the tiny waist that flares out to well-rounded hips and a chest that would struggle to reach mine in size but is sexy and plump, with a cleavage that could drown any man's desires.

Feeling decidedly in the way, I scrape back my chair and say quickly, "I should head to my desk, it's going to be a long day."

They look up in surprise, telling me they've forgotten I was even here, and it makes me smile. They really do have it all and as they smile sweetly as I leave, I don't think I've ever been so jealous of two people and what they have in my life before.

CHAPTER 33

DEXTER

*W*e head to the den and Sam looks worried. "What's up?"

In a low voice, I tell him what my cryptic text revealed.

"It appears they have our man."

"Holly's stepbrother?"

"Yes, he showed up at his mom's house yesterday evening. Ryder's team went in and now he's safely locked up at The Rubicon awaiting interrogation."

Sam shivers. "That doesn't sound good—for him."

"Only if he withholds the information we want."

"What about her old man, isn't he some military sergeant or something? I'm guessing he didn't just sit back and let them take his stepson."

"Actually, he was the one who tipped them off."

Sam looks so surprised I almost laugh out loud. Lowering my voice, I whisper, "Holly's father is a loyal officer. He was told his son was involved with terrorists and needed to be lifted out of the situation for his own protection. His commanding officer told him everything we wanted him to know and so when Colton showed up unannounced, intent on staying only one hour, Ryder got the call to strike and so, here we are, one step closer to finding out what the hell is going on."

Sam falls silent, and I know he has many questions. He never asks the full story, just knows that I belong to an organization that involves several top CEOs and powerful men. He knows I have a job to do but knows nothing of the King himself. Do any of us really? It's that thought that worries me because life is changing for all of us and we may not like what that means.

As soon as we reach my den, Sam waits for instruction and as I read the text that I'm surprised to see, I smile. "It appears our stay here is at an end. Maybe you should make the necessary arrangements."

"And Miss. Bryant?"

"Move her things to my apartment."

Sam raises his eyes and I nod, feeling very pleased with how this day is going already.

"Yes, she is now my new apprentice in every way. New beginnings Sam, and uncertain endings."

Shaking his head, he grins. "I'm happy for you, Dexter. I hope it all works out."

"What you mean is, you hope I don't fuck this up."

I roll my eyes as he laughs and as he leaves, I turn my attention to the text I received at breakfast.

Reaching for my phone, I make the call and wonder what this all means for Holly.

"Hey, you took your time."

"Says you, what's up, Ryder, you losing your touch? I've been kicking my heels here for well over a week already."

"I expect you've kept yourself busy."

"You know me so well."

He laughs softly and then a more serious tone creeps into his voice.

"We've been ghosted."

"Meaning?"

"Holly's stepbrother is an impressive technician. He's been oper-ating a dual set up to ours, existing under the radar. Twinned our systems and cloned our codes. This man has been playing us like puppets this entire time and if I wasn't so pissed, I'd sign him up."

"Then why don't you?"

He chuckles. *"He may not feel like accepting the job."*

"He's bad then."

"What do you think?"

Part of me feels bad for Holly, but this man must have known what he was dealing with when he started and I guard my words carefully.

"Is he working alone?"

"No."

Ryder's answer is abrupt and I know better than to ask the name of the actual person responsible, so I say in a lighter tone, "And Holly?"

"Needs to know nothing. She can continue as normal."

Thinking about Holly and the many questions she will surely have, Ryder must read my mind because he says quickly, *"Just tell her he's helping us solve the problem. She doesn't need to know the details. Thank her and move on, it's best that way."*

"What if I can't move on? What if I've made her an offer she's already accepted? I had to get the information somehow. It didn't come cheap either."

Ryder laughs and I can picture his smirk from here.

"Then enjoy what you paid so well for."

For some reason, I don't like the thought that I paid for Holly. It doesn't seem right, but isn't that exactly what happened. She's only here for what I can give her, and I don't like how that makes me feel.

So I bite and snap, "Fuck you, Ryder, keep me posted."

I cut the call and turn my head to business. I can't think

about that conversation for a moment longer because if I do, I would hate myself even more than I do already. Like everything in my life, the people in it are only there because I pay them to be.

CHAPTER 34

HOLLY

I wish I never heard that comment. I could hear Dexter on the phone the moment I reached the den. Shamelessly, I stood outside and heard him tell whoever was on the other end of the line that he had paid for my information. He did what was necessary to get what he wanted and if I felt cheap before, it's nothing to how I feel now. This is all a business transaction to him. Emotionless bastard and if anything, he did warn me. He doesn't want me—just my body. He doesn't care about the woman inside and has just used the situation to his advantage.

What do I do now?

It goes against every bone in my body to open the door and smile brightly as he looks up when I enter.

"Hey."

He nods. "Come and sit down, baby, I have news."

If anything, his endearing name for me just makes my skin crawl because now I can see it's all an act. He bought me, plain and simple, and when he gets bored, he'll figure out a way to get rid just as easily.

"I think work can take a back seat for a few hours."

My heart sinks. He has that look in his eyes that tells me he's not done playing with me yet and I wonder what sick pleasure he has thought up this morning.

"You want fresh air, allow me to oblige."

I look up in shock. "You mean we can go outside?"

"Yes, baby, let me show you why I love it here so much."

I could be forgiven for thinking that everything was ok because he has an excitement surrounding him that's contagious. But I know what I heard and I don't like it at all, but I need to park it and consider my options before I make any decisions that may blow up in my face.

He reaches for my hand and as it closes around mine, I could weep tears of disappointment and frustration. Why can't I have it all? What have I done to be treated like this because I would never play with anyone's feelings the way he loves playing with mine?

We head back to our respective rooms to change and for the first time in a while, I pull on my jeans and a t-shirt. Tying my hair up in a ponytail, I reach for my boots as instructed.

As I walk to meet him, it feels strange without my heels because now I'm smaller and more vulnerable in every way.

When I head into the kitchen Dexter is already waiting and if I thought Jason looked good as a cowboy, it's nothing to the one standing before me now. It suits him. Dexter does rough extremely well and I struggle so hard to keep my poker face on because I don't want him to know how much I desire him. He's cocky enough, but fuck me, the sight of that body stuffed into a cowboy shirt and those jeans failing to disguise the extra passenger he always carries in his pants is sending me delirious.

He has his own cowboy hat and boots and I clench my legs to stop an extremely embarrassing wet patch from showing because this man will be the death of every principle I own.

He reaches for my hand and I follow him outside and see the jeep waiting with a beaming Jason inside.

"Hey guys, I've got the horses ready and Maisy's packed a picnic, enjoy."

Dexter pulls me in beside him and as we set off down the track, the jeep bumps over the rough ground, shaking my bones, making me cling onto Dexter for support.

He leans down and whispers, "I know the perfect spot to rip those clothes off your back because honey, you are about to go on the ride of your life."

I have no words. No powers at all because he has broken me. As fantasies go, this one will not go unplayed because, despite how I feel, I'm interested to see where this leads, then I'll deal with it. Maybe leave, tear up the contract, make a stand.

You're a fool.

That voice is already mocking me because even she knows there is no way in hell I'm going anywhere.

Summer's the pretty white horse they have given me and I fall in love with her on sight. As I stroke her nose and press kisses on her skin, she neighs appreciatively and nuzzles my hand.

Dexter looks impressed. "She likes you."

"Treat a girl well and she'll love you forever."

He shakes his head as Jason laughs. "True enough, darlin', the biggest lesson a guy could ever learn."

Dexter doesn't appear to listen to advice because he's more intent on stroking his own horse's mane and making him feel like his one and only, and he probably is. Now I'm jealous of a fucking horse which shows me how far I've fallen and feeling slightly irritable, I pull myself up into the saddle and Jason says with admiration, "Looks like you've done this before."

"Junior champion at Clover-falls academy. Boarding school had its advantages."

Jason grins and tosses me a hat and as I pull it down on my

head, I catch Dexter looking at me with a very strange expression that sends a tingle down my spine. There's a deep yearning in the stare that vanishes almost as soon as it appeared and if I had blinked at the wrong moment, I would have missed it.

He swings onto his own horse and Jason says, "I'll set up your picnic at the creek. Then some of us have work to do."

He laughs as Dexter grins. "Some of us have to keep the world spinning, thanks man."

As Jason heads off in a cloud of dust, Summer seems impatient to get off and I know the feeling because looking at Dexter Prince sitting on top of a pure black stallion is a sight I will never forget.

"You ready, baby, I'll go slow if you need me to?"

Gritting my teeth, I pull on Summer's reins and say icily, "Don't you dare."

Laughing, he heads off and if what happened to me was worth anything, it's this moment. It all comes together in the most exhilarating way as I follow Dexter across fields that settle inside a landscape of outstanding natural beauty. The sun is hot, but the breeze is fine and as we gallop over the dusty ground, I have never felt so alive.

CHAPTER 35

DEXTER

*R*yder's call made me feel like a bastard. I just swept his comment under the rug, but it's still there taunting me. When I saw Holly Bryant at Media Corp, I wanted her. To conquer her and to watch her begging for me on her knees. Most of that has come true already, but now I know her. I love that she will never beg. She's strong, resilient and has a beautiful soul that I'm a bastard for not exploring further. But she will never be any more than that to me. How could she be because I have set cast-iron rules in place to guard my heart?

As she rides her mare, I appreciate the view. Not the beautiful one surrounding us, but her. The wild, spirited woman who is close to breaking point. I can see it in her eyes. Something has changed between us. She almost looks resigned to playing my prisoner and I don't like it—at all.

So, I'm setting her free in a sense. Giving her the fresh air she craves and spending a pleasant afternoon of my own. The picnic was a stroke of genius because I need her to want to stay so I can sleep without fear she'll be gone in the morning. It's time to give her a reason to stay, as Jason so bluntly put it, and I hope it's not too late.

I direct the horses to a clearing on the edge of Picket Point. The part of my property that ceases being maintained and nature is allowed to rule with a free hand. Jumping down from my horse, I shout, "We can lead them through the trees, there's a clearing with water for them and our picnic should be waiting."

Once again, I thank Jason for being a good friend and as we duck and move through the trees, it takes all my concentration to remember the way.

By the time the trees open up, Saracen whinnies and I laugh softly, "Easy boy, you've earned your rest."

Holly gasps behind me and I can see why because Picket Point is the bold strokes of Nature at her finest. A sparkling lake surrounded by trees with a 360-degree scene of beauty. Jason has set up a picnic on a plaid rug and even managed to stuff a cooler with a bottle of champagne to accompany the much-needed water.

"Wow, Dexter, this place is so beautiful."

"Yes, I'll not argue with that."

Tethering Saracen to the purpose-built wooden frame, I take Holly's horse and give him a beautiful companion to keep him company. They have enough rope to drink from the lake and seem happy to have a brief moment of rest after the ride through the blistering sun.

Slinging down my hat, I wipe my brow and groan. "I should do that more often. I'm out of practise."

Holly tosses her own hat to mine and releases her hair from the ponytail and runs her fingers through it. "I'm so hot."

She sure is and I can't help myself and say almost immediately, "Then take off your clothes."

"What here?"

"Obviously here." I reach for my own shirt and pull it off,

loving how she can't appear to look anywhere else. I make short work of my pants and soon stand before her with nothing but an extremely interested cock pointing her way.

Without another word, her clothes soon follow mine and I nod toward the lake.

"I think we should cool off."

"Is it safe?"

Looking at the clear, crystal water sparking in the rays of sunshine that filter through the canopy of trees, I grin. "Not entirely."

"Why, are there snakes, because I absolutely will not go anywhere I think I may be bitten by a snake?"

She looks genuinely afraid and I laugh. "There's only one snake that concerns you baby and it's all yours to pet at will."

She blushes and yet her eyes sparkle as she looks at my cock with a mixture of lust and fear because she knows she won't escape what I have planned and the unknown is a delicious sense of expectation hanging in the air between us.

To break the tension, she leaps into the lake and her squeals echo around the clearing because it's damned cold in there. I know that first-hand and I laugh as she splutters as she surfaces, looking shocked. "You never told me it was like Antarctica in here. I'm going to die."

"Then I had better save you."

Jumping in, I love the shock this place always gives my body because it electrifies my senses and recharges my soul. As I swim toward her, she stares at me with a longing that tells me I have her hooked on my line and as I reach for her, I pull her in for a bruising kiss of mass destruction. Our lips clash and tongues collide and as her arms wrap around me, I love the feeling of her wet tits pressing into my chest and when her legs wrap around my waist, I almost groan with longing because she will test all the control I pride myself on because I want nothing more than to spend the rest of the day inside her glorious body.

We kiss, we explore under water and we swim and only when we drag ourselves out to the bank, do we get down to the business I brought her here for.

As she shivers on the rug, I say darkly, "Lie on your back and look up at me."

She lies back and I drag my lustful gaze over her glorious body and growl, "Spread your legs."

She licks her lip nervously and does as I say and as I stroke my cock, her eyes widen as the length increases and I kneel between her legs and rub slowly and firmly while staring into her eyes. It's like I'm masturbating over a centerfold and I say huskily, "Play with yourself."

She looks mortified and like the wicked bastard I am, I say roughly, "Don't displease me, baby, I want to see you give yourself pleasure while I watch."

Slowly she moves her fingers to her clit and after a few embarrassed tries, soon gets into it and as she closes her eyes, I snap, "Eyes on me."

They snap open and soon we are staring into each other's eyes, giving ourselves pleasure while the other watches. To me, she has never looked more beautiful. Her cheeks are flushed, her hair wet, the droplets of water still clinging to her lashes and coating her skin. Her moans drive me on and as she wriggles beneath her own hand, I pump faster as the sticky trail between her legs coats her fingers.

"Suck your fingers, one by one."

She nods, and it's almost unbearable as she slowly sucks each one of those sticky fingers while holding my gaze. As I pump, she plays and as her breath hitches and her pupils dilate, I know she close and like the wicked bastard I am I say, "Enough."

She looks confused as I say roughly, "You will not come, now sit up and face me."

The confusion in her eyes excites me as she sits up and I say darkly, "Kneel."

I always knew she would follow instruction perfectly and seeing her kneeling on the rug waiting to do whatever I say causes the power to blind me to what's right. I own her, she's mine. I can do whatever the fuck I want and I love how that makes me feel.

CHAPTER 36

HOLLY

*H*e proves over and over again what a bastard he is. Creating a beautiful intimate moment and then ruining it in an offhand way.

As I kneel facing him, I wonder what game he is playing, but I can't deny how excited it makes me feel. It's the unknown. Not knowing what he's going to do next that turns me on so badly and as he reaches into the cooler and opens a bottle of water, I love how he holds it to my lips and says gently, "Drink this."

I make to take the bottle and he growls, "No hands, I will do it for you."

As he feeds me water like a mother nursing a child, I hate to admit I love it. Maybe it's the care in his eyes as I gulp down the cool water, realizing how dehydrated I was.

I almost drain the bottle and as he pulls it away, he wipes my lips with his mouth. Sucking in my lower lip and biting it gently, causing a delicious shiver of lust to pass through my body.

Still holding my gaze, he reaches into the cooler and removes one of his own and says, "Feed me."

As I return the favor, my hands shake as I hold the bottle at an angle to help him drink and as he finishes, he reaches out and strokes my hair lovingly, much like he did his horse and whispers, "Thank you, angel."

This tender side of him hurts my heart because I rarely see it and crave it more than anything. His fingers drift lazily down my chest and he circles a nipple and twists it sharply, causing a sudden burst of pain to shatter the sweet moment. I know what he's doing, reminding me who's in charge here, and I'm not sure if it's for my benefit or his. Because that yearning in my heart is mirrored right back at me through his eyes and it appears that Dexter Prince is struggling to control his own emotions, which does give me some hope at least.

Breaking the spell, he says almost casually, "We should eat, you must be starving."

"I am." I can't ignore how empty I feel in every way and as he reaches into the basket, I feel like Adam and Eve in the Garden of Eden as he pulls out sandwiches and fruit and hands me my share.

We sit in silence eating our food, falling into an easy companionship as we admire the view. After a while, he says gently, "Are you happy, baby?"

"Not really."

He looks at me sharply, and I shrug. "How can I be happy when I'm here under these circumstances? I'm not unhappy though, which shows how fucked my mind is."

"Not really, I understand that feeling more than anyone."

He seems thoughtful and sighs. "To the outside world, I have it all. Power, money, and anything I want is at my disposable. But there's a lot missing that can't be bought."

"Such as."

I'm not sure if he's even going to answer me, but to my surprise, says huskily, "I don't have my sister, my family or someone to come home to at night. Someone who loves the man, not the media giant. It's something I deny myself because I don't deserve it. I wrecked the one person I love in the world and took away her future. Me, Holly, I did that and so I must live a cold empty life to make up for it."

"She wouldn't want that."

My voice sounds nervous and almost a whisper, as if I don't have the right to challenge him and he nods.

"You're right, she would tell me I'm an ass and to go and live my best life because she was a good person. A happy soul who only wanted the best for everyone. I couldn't bear to watch that spirit destroyed by a man like Mario Cordoli. He would break her, drive desperation into her life, and ruin the girl I loved with all my heart. Turns out I was the real problem and did that, anyway."

He seems so broken my heart shatters and reaching out, I take his hand and lean against him, my head on his shoulder. "You have to forgive yourself, Dexter. You say you have power, everything you want, but won't allow yourself a future filled with happiness. It will drive you mad and all the people who rely on you, Sam, Jason, Maisy, Saracen over there, Media Corp and whatever else you have your finger dipped into. They are all real, Dexter and would miss you terribly if you self-destructed. Honor your sister's memory by living your best life. You said yourself she would want that for you. Let her soul live in peace because I'm guessing she's as worried about you as the rest of the people who love you."

Maybe I've gone too far because I doubt anyone's ever spoken to him like this and as he said himself, he's a dominant and won't appreciate my bold words.

Then he says softly, "I don't want to talk about me, baby. I'm not an interesting subject. I want to know what you want the most and it better not be your freedom."

He winks and makes out it's a joke, but I can see the edge of uncertainty in his eyes that tells me he's afraid. For some reason, that makes me hurt even more because it appears he doesn't want to let me in but doesn't want me to leave either.

So, I decide to lighten the atmosphere and say almost wistfully, "I want to be like Maisy. Have the love of a good man who loves her and dedicate my life to him. An easy life filled with laughter, love, and hard work. I want someone to make love to me as if I'm the most beautiful woman in the world. I just want to feel that once at least."

He turns and throws me a look that could torch a mountain and whispers, "Then let's make that wish come true, for one day only."

Reaching out, he strokes my face lightly and I melt inside as my breath hitches at the look of love in his eyes. Then he cups my face and gently kisses my lips as if I'm the rarest treasure and his kiss is soft, hesitant, almost as if he's afraid I'll break. The dominant has gone and in his place is a man with so much love to give and the realization of that momentarily blinds me. As we kiss, the birds cry overhead as they witness nature at her finest.

Pressing me down onto the rug, his hands trace a tantalizing path down my body as he kisses me with more passion and an urgency I match in every way.

I shiver beneath him as he presses in harder and I moan in anticipation of something I never dared hope for—him.

Now I have free rein and allow my own hands to explore and love how every touch and gentle rub causes him to groan and tense under my touch.

As I start my own explorations, I relish every taste of him because as I lick, kiss and suck every inch of his body, I love how good he tastes. Reaching for his cock, I lick the tip that spills pre-cum on my tongue and he lies like stone beneath me as gently I take him in and slide it to the back of my throat. As I cup his balls in my hand with care and reverence, I gently squeeze as I suck and lick, loving the way he groans louder the more I tease him.

Without waiting for permission, I pull away and, sitting astride him, I stare deep into his eyes and as I lower myself onto that weapon of mass destruction, I gasp as it slides into my core, grazing my walls and marking me as his. It's a delicious feeling as he fills me and owns my body and as we stare deep into each other's eyes, I know I'm not the only one affected by this.

He grips my waist and reaching up, takes my breast into his mouth and sucks hard, causing me to gasp with pleasure as I gently rock on his cock.

He transfers his attention to the other one and I moan softly as I move carefully up and down his shaft, loving how he fills me so completely.

Then he leans back and whispers, "This feels so good."

"It does." I lean down, kissing him gently as he fills the whole of me. For a moment we are so close not a bead of sweat could slide between us and as I move gently on top of my cowboy, I finally know what it's all about. Sex without love is nowhere near as powerful as making love to a man you couldn't want more, and I do want the man, not the dominant because he is a far more interesting character than the cold, unfeeling, sexy dominant, who has opened up a new world to me in a destructive way.

He pushes me onto my back and the atmosphere changes. Becomes more anxious, less relaxed as he increases his pace. My legs wrap around him and pull him in deeper and as he thrusts, the excitement builds as he fucks me so hard, I can only see him. It feels like hot pleasure racing through my entire body as he pounds harder, deeper and with powerful strokes. All the time he looks into my eyes and it blows my mind. He is relentless and as his fingers pinch my throbbing clit, I scream so hard I disturb the horses and then a miracle happens because as I come so hard I see stars, so does he and his release is like the roar of a lion as he empties his seed inside my body in one powerful burst of pleasure.

We come down together, our hands entwined and feeling so powerful it's a difficult drug to kick. He pulls me hard against him and as his arms fold around me, pulling me even closer, I hear the frantic beat of his heart as he gives me the whole of him for the first time.

As my eyes close, I feel the tears spill because I got my wish. I have never felt so loved in my life, and he gave me the world right then. If only it was mine to keep.

CHAPTER 37

DEXTER

*T*his feels so different. Losing control to Holly is not as bad as I thought it would be and for the first time in many years, I could almost forget everything that ties me to a lifetime of decisions, regret, and trying to do the right thing. This *is* the right thing—for today, anyway, and I just enjoy a carefree time that has appeared out of nowhere.

Releasing into Holly was long overdue because it wasn't just my seed that left me, it was tension. It felt so good to lose it for one brief moment and as I held her shaking body against mine; I thank God for sending her to me.

Today is different in every way and I owe her that at least, so once we clean up and dress, I take her hand and pull her close for a long, deep, passionate kiss.

"Thank you." I whisper against her mouth and she says, "I should be thanking you; you gave me my dream."

"It was my pleasure, ma'am."

I adopt a slow drawl and raise my hat to her and she giggles, transforming her usual guarded expression into one of joy and beauty.

She is absolutely breath-taking and I could stare at her all day long, but instead we mount our horses and head back at a more leisurely pace.

As we ride side by side, it feels good showing her my rustic kingdom. I point out places of interest along the way and it feels good sharing this place with her.

When we make it back to the yard, one of the hands appears to take our horses and as we reward them both with a pat and a fistful of hay, I love how that makes me feel. It feels good to give pleasure of a more natural kind. Seeing Holly's bright smile and hearing her laugh makes me feel good about myself for once.

I decide to walk back to the house and as we set off hand in hand, it all feels so natural.

"This has been an amazing day, thank you."

Holly's soft voice interrupts my thinking and I smile.

"It has."

"So, what happens next, obviously something's changed. Is it Colton?"

She looks anxious and I wonder if she's been holding this in all day and feel a little bad for her because she won't like what she hears and it could ruin the mood.

Choosing my words carefully, I say firmly, "Your stepbrother is helping with our enquiries. Your job is done and now we can start the next stage."

"Is he ok?" Her voice shakes and picturing the state he's probably in right now, I say darkly, "I have no reason to think otherwise."

"But you don't know for sure."

"No, baby, I don't but whatever happens is because he made it that way. Don't worry about your stepbrother because he certainly didn't offer you the same courtesy when he got you involved in this."

She falls silent and after a while, says timidly, "What happens when we leave?"

"We head back to Media Corp and your new life. Your belongings are being taken to my apartment in the city and your job is waiting as my apprentice. Helen, my assistant, is making that happen and so, first thing tomorrow, we go to work."

Once again, she is silent and I wonder what's running through her mind right now and then she shocks me by squeezing my hand tightly and saying, "I'm afraid, Dexter."

"Of what?" Spinning around, I lift her face to look at mine and see the doubt crowding her gorgeous eyes. "What's the matter, baby, this is what you wanted?"

"I thought I did, but now..." She tails off and I'm genuinely confused. "Do you regret this?"

I'm almost fearful of the answer as she shakes her head and her eyes fill with tears. "I will never regret this—experience. I suppose it's the unknown that's scaring me. I want to be the best, to work hard and make a name for myself, but I'm starting to realize the name I'll make is probably not one I want to be called by."

"What do you mean?" I run my thumb over her lips and smile into her eyes because, for some reason, I want to comfort the usually strong woman who looks so scared of something.

"I will be known as the woman who slept her way into her position. They will all hate me and look at me as if I'm not worth their time because I have been plucked from the bottom to be by your side. I haven't earned it."

Leaning down, I kiss her lips and whisper, "You have."

Breaking away, she says angrily, "Exactly. I've earned it on my back, just like they will think. You say it was the information that got me the job, that doesn't make it any better. I sold my family for personal gain. I did everything you asked of me and now I have to live with what I did it for."

"So, what do you want, Holly, because I'm struggling to see what's wrong about this?"

"I don't know." She sighs and I can tell she's struggling.

"I suppose I just want to feel proud of my achievements. Know I got there the right way because of how good I am at the job, not in the sack. How can I move past this, Dexter because I do want this opportunity, but I'm not sure if I can bear the look in their eyes when they pass?"

"Who are we talking about here, Holly? Who are 'they' you fear so much? Let me tell you, they are no different from you. Anyone would have done what you did, but the difference is they weren't given that opportunity. You say you went from the bottom to the top - wrong. You have just changed desks because if you want this badly enough, you will have to prove to me and them, whoever they are, that you are worth it. So, dry your tears, push away those doubts and sharpen those killer heels you love because no apprentice of mine doesn't start the day with fire and determination to succeed and fuck the lot of them. Prove you are meant to be there and they will soon admire you for what you can do. Do I make myself clear, Holly Bryant, this is in your hands, fight for it?"

I fix her with my darkest look and she responds by tossing away her doubts and facing me with a different look in her eye.

"Thanks, sir, I needed that."

Pulling her angrily toward me, I punish those lips for daring to have self-doubt and as I push in against her, she runs her hands under my shirt and rakes those nails down my back, and I feel like the most powerful man alive.

Pushing her roughly against a nearby tree, I say darkly, "Wrap your arms around that tree."

Her breath labors as she does what I say and with one sharp move, I rip down her jeans and toss them to the side. Her panties follow.

Then I kick those legs apart and whisper, "Remember the second part of our deal, baby, remember I own you at night."

"Yes, sir."

As I pull out my cock, I stroke the shaft and relish the sight in front of me. Mine. My woman in every way and with a feral growl, I impale her from behind and her gasp of surprise fuels my passion as I pound into her again and again as I remind her who's in charge now. Reaching down, I squeeze her clit and as she screams so hard, I empty my seed inside her for the second time today. It's basic, raw and edged in depravity and I love how she can match me and take everything I throw at her.

Grabbing her hair, I yank her head back, still inside her and growl, "Do you feel how much I want you, Holly? How much I own every part of you and how much I can give you? This is what you want and you will soon realize that. You are *my* woman, and I expect you to be strong. Don't let me down."

She cries out as I bite her neck and says breathlessly, "Thank you, sir."

Just hearing her soft voice say what I needed to hear, I spin her around and kiss her with a desperation I never knew I had. Why do I need her so badly and just the thought of any doubts in her mind sends me into a control frenzy? How can someone like Holly make me lose my mind at the thought of her leaving me?

As we arrange our clothing and head back to the ranch, both of us are preoccupied. A new beginning awaits, which I'm excited for, but I know I don't have any of the control I seek because if Holly hates every minute of it, she will leave and I'm not sure how I feel about that.

CHAPTER 38

HOLLY

A day of mixed emotions that takes some sorting.

Dexter has been different today and showed me a side to him that is almost human. I prefer it, in fact. The softer, more vulnerable, yet playful side to a man with more layers than anyone I've ever known.

Tonight, we eat dinner with his staff, or as I thought, friends. Jason, Maisy and Sam sit around the table and it's an easy atmosphere.

Dexter is less guarded with them. Wicked banter passes around the table like the dishes that are laden with delicious food, lovingly prepared by Maisy.

I love every part of this. Never having the whole family meal thing going on, I am eager to appreciate every fine minute of this one, despite the fact it's a strange mixture of family, friend and employment status.

It strikes me that we are all here to play some part in Dexter's Prince's life. His bodyguard and best friend, who undoubtedly has his full loyalty. They have an easy relationship and it's good to see. Maisy and Jason keep his beloved ranch running and provide home comforts when he needs it. Then there's me. His sex slave and apprentice all rolled into one. And I'm still not sure how I feel about that.

Seeing Maisy and Jason and the obvious loving relationship they share creates a deep yearning inside me for one of my own.

I want this. The dream. Then again, I want the power, the empire and the career. Above all of this, though, I want the man and it's that crashing realization that shocks me the most. Why do I want him? I still don't know, but there's something about him that pulls me in and devours me whole because life without him would be nowhere near as interesting.

I help Maisy clean the dishes and she whispers, "Good day?" She winks and I wonder if it's so obvious because ever since our picnic, I've been walking on air.

"It was good thanks."

I grin and she nudges me playfully. "It's good to see him happy. You make him happy, Holly, I just want you to know that."

"Do I, I'm not so sure?"

"Take it from a gal who sees from the outside. That man is hard to read but lately he looks almost human."

"Now I know you're lying."

We giggle and I say enviously, "How long have you been married?"

"Oh honey…" she giggles. "Jason and me ain't married. We just live each day as it comes and I'm more than happy about that."

"Seriously, but I thought…" I feel a little shocked by that and she laughs softly. "I love the brute, but marriage is way off. We were childhood sweethearts, but the road ended past school finishing and hooking up again. You see, honey, Jason took me for granted for a very long time. He thought I was always going to be there and didn't care about my feelings. I found out he cheated on me when he was out of town and it wasn't the first time."

Now my mouth drops open and she sighs, staring out of the window at the brightly star lit sky.

"For a while there, we went our separate ways. I made a few mistakes myself and tried to live a different life, but when we met by chance one day, those old memories flooded back and after a while we started dating again."

"You forgave him, that must have taken a lot."

"Honey, when something is right, and it takes a while for you both to see it, past actions have no bearing on the future. Jason was sorry. I was forgiving and we both know it can never happen again. It's why we live like this, no rings to bind us, just desire. We both want it but don't want to take it for granted, and that is why every single time he asks me, I refuse."

"To marry him."

She nods. "Yes, you see I never want him to stop trying to keep me."

She smiles brightly. "Anyway, I'll make some coffee, go and spend time with your man, I'll bring it over."

"He's not…" She winks. "He is, you just don't know it yet— either of you."

Dexter smiles as I approach and it takes my breath away. I'm not used to seeing this side of him. The one where he is relaxed and, dare I say it, almost normal. A man like him can never be normal, that's definite, but the lazy way he drags his eyes over my body with a sense of ownership, I'm ashamed to admit, turns me on and makes me almost think this might work.

I look at Jason a little differently as I sit beside Dexter and he pulls me in to his side. The guys are playing cards and it feels good to be here. Part of a small intimate gathering with no stress or need to play a part.

Dexter has a shot of whiskey by his side and his cards in one hand, me in the other, and I love it.

I don't even bother to understand what game they're playing because cards have always bored me senseless. Instead, I snuggle up to him and imagine a time when this was actually real. Dexter was my husband, even. We have a family of our own and, as the delightful dream claims my consciousness, I drift off to sleep.

It's only when I hear a gentle, "Baby, it's time for bed." do I stir and blearily look around me and notice we're alone.

"Wow, I'm sorry, I must have fallen asleep."

"You don't say." He laughs and pulls me up with him.

"Come on, we've a full day ahead tomorrow and you need to be on your A game."

As we walk to our rooms, I fully expect him to kiss me at my door as usual, but am surprised when he whispers, "Will you stay with me tonight?"

"Are you sure?" I think I must still be dreaming, and he nods. "I'm not ready to let you go yet."

My heart sinks because that's all this is to him, probably another sex marathon where he demonstrates how much he owns me. Sighing inside, I nod, "Ok."

We head past my room to his at the end of the hall and as he opens the door, I gasp when I see the candles burning on surfaces everywhere.

"Dexter, I mean…"

"Dexter's fine, Holly. Here at my ranch, I want you to feel comfortable. For us to have a different kind of relationship away from the city one."

"What do you mean?" I am genuinely confused, and he pulls me close and smiles. "I want to meet you half way. I know how much you want the whole fairy story—to have it all. I also know I can't give you that, but here—I can."

Stroking my face, he kisses my lips sweetly and softly and

says huskily, "Here, we can be different. Relax and enjoy a basic life with no expectations other than enjoying our time here together. This will be our home together, Holly. When we return to the city, I will be your boss and your dominant. What do you say, would that work for you?"

For some reason, my eyes fill with tears because I know how hard this was for him. He can't give me emotion, yet he has already proven it's inside him banging on the lid to get out. He is scared though, backing away as soon as it surfaces and I suppose this is the best I can expect, so I nod, "I think it would."

As Dexter tastes my lips for the thousandth time today, it feels a little different now. I feel like his equal and as we slowly remove our clothes, I know this time will be different too. An extension of our picnic because when he wants to be, Dexter can be the perfect lover that brims with emotion and it's up to both of us to meet in the middle somehow.

CHAPTER 39

DEXTER

*T*he helicopter circles the ranch and I feel a pang of regret as we wave to Maisy and Jason, who stand watching us go. Every time I leave this place, I am already planning my return, but life always gets in the way.

This time I have Holly beside me and Sam beside the pilot and I can't imagine this ever changing. I have it all, at least I think I do, and as much as I loved waking up in Holly's arms this morning, I know I will not allow a repeat when we return to the city. I can't because then I would be breaking my own rules and opening past wounds that have never really healed.

Holly is excited but nervous and just being in the helicopter is something I doubt she has ever experienced and so I spend the journey explaining the places we pass over and answer her questions. The more time I spend with her, the more I enjoy her company because she has a quick wit and is always asking intelligent questions.

As soon as we touch down on the helipad at Media Corp, I feel the pressure return and watch as everything happens like clockwork as we are met by Helen who is waiting with my two security guards.

Helen looks at Holly with interest, and I'm guessing she has many questions that will never receive a direct answer. Only Holly needs to know the details of our relationship and so I leave her to scramble after me as we leave the helicopter and deliver her to Helen to take under her wing.

If Holly's surprised at my lack of attention, she hides it well and I don't give her a backward glance as I head inside my empire and prepare to rule.

My head of security whispers in my ear and I feel the anticipation build as he fills me in.

My security team follow me and Helen and Holly bring up the rear with Sam walking a discreet distance in front.

My entourage. They always surround me and as I step into my private elevator that takes me straight to my executive suite of offices, I love the feeling this place gives me. It wraps me up in destiny and allows me to make the world a better place, or worse, depending if you're on the receiving end of a very bad day at the office.

As soon as I step out of the elevator, I know he's here. Easy enough to guess when I see the bastards he brought with him littering my visitor's area. Dirty bikers with more tattoos than skin and a fuck-off attitude that scares the fuck out of my staff.

Leaving Sam to organize the chaos, I head into my office and say roughly, "Help yourself, why don't you?"

Ryder is sitting in front of my desk with a shot of whiskey, studying his phone, and an arrogant grin breaks out across his face when he sees me enter the room.

"What time is this to come to work, man you're losing your grip?

"Who says I haven't been working?"

I drop into my seat and grin. "Good to see you, what's the news?"

"I thought that was your speciality."

"It is but as we know, you're the one that makes it for me, so what's the story with Holly's stepbrother and who the fuck is trying to bring our organization down?"

I am excited to discover what he knows and he shrugs. "I know who it isn't."

"Seriously, Ryder, you've come all this way to tell me what I already know. Don't make me hate you more than I already do."

He laughs and raises his glass. "Turns out Colton was trained in ghosting our systems. He was an IT major and excelled at university. He was head-hunted for a rival organization to ours who have been ghosting us for months. Tapping into our phones, computers and records. All the time under an invisibility cloak that you can only find if you know it's there. Impressive."

"It sure is. So now?"

"It's been ghosted right back. Colton bargained for his life by showing Brewer how it worked. He had the passwords necessary to divert the information to a different server. The person responsible doesn't know the information we are now feeding them is what we put there with a specific purpose in mind. Our usual information has been filtered through a different server, one that this organization has no access to and so the hunter is now the hunted as we play a game of cat and mouse."

I lean back and reach for the whiskey myself because this is serious shit. "And Holly's parents. What do they know, does she need to pay them a visit?"

"I doubt it. Her father's already back in the field and her stepmother is cheering herself up in the South of France. Caring bastards, aren't they?"

I feel my insides twist with rage when I think of Holly being treated by her family as disposable. She has absolutely no one who cares for her and I don't like how that makes me feel inside. Pushing that aside for later, I snarl,

"So, who is behind it and don't fucking tell me you don't know."

"I don't know."

Ryder grins as I throw up my hands and shout, "Are you fucking serious?"

"Like I said, I know who it isn't, and that's the four of us."

My blood runs cold. "So, the fifth...?"

"It all points to him."

For a moment, we pause and allow the enormity of our situation to sink in. The King. The actual fucking King. It doesn't make sense.

"What now?" I feel defeated before I even ask the question because if he wants us out of the picture, we had better start packing or planning our funerals.

"We go to the wedding as planned."

"And what is the plan when this shit blows up in our faces?"

"I'm working on that."

"Well, work hard, my friend, because time is most definitely running out. The weddings in a few days, for Christ's sake."

"Which is a good thing because we have a few days head start."

For some reason, the grim determination on his face settles my jagged nerves and I sigh heavily. "What do you need me to do?"

He leans back in his seat and smiles. "Put on a suit, order some flowers and call the gift company because nothing has changed. We go to the wedding and act as we always have done."

Nodding, I throw him my usual smirk. "Do you even own a suit?"

He laughs. "I may have one gathering dust in my closet."

"And the other kings, do they know?"

"Of course. We go separately as planned and meet at the

wedding. Keep to protocol, do what we have to do and hope it all blows up in our faces."

"That's your plan?" Shaking my head, I grab my glass and empty it in one gulp and Ryder grins. "It's what I hope will happen."

"And you will do…"

"Nothing."

"Great, how can this plan ever fail, we're all going to die?"

He laughs. "I said *I'm* doing nothing, there's a difference."

Sighing, I know there's nothing much coming my way from him, anyway, and as he stands, he nods. "Thanks for the drink. Now it's been nice, but we need to return home and pack."

"I'm honored you came all this way to tell me in person."

"I had business in the area and anyway, you know that's how it works, trust no one…"

"And never betray that trust."

I finish our motto and he grins. "Until the big event."

He leaves and I watch the door close and think about what he said.

Two days head start, that's not good odds. Things are moving so fast and somebody wants us gone. We are like cattle to slaughter and now our motto needs to stand up and be counted because if we've only got a few more days to live, God help us and all that we stand for.

CHAPTER 40

HOLLY

*H*elen seems nice. A little aloof perhaps, but calm and professional. She takes me to human resources and signs me up, security passes, endless forms, and then a guided tour of the building.

This place is nothing like The Globe. Much better. More luxurious, with a different kind of atmosphere. Professional people, desperate to succeed, unlike the attention-grabbing journalists I have come to know and hate. I wonder what they would say if they saw where I was now? I doubt they would believe their eyes, because I certainly don't.

I've arrived. It certainly feels that way and I don't miss the curious stares of the people that work here as they watch the new girl being shown around by none other than the big man's assistant. They will be wondering who I am and I feel my breath coming fast as the anxiety comes along for the ride. What possessed me to think I was good enough for this? To work among seasoned professionals who took years to make it to this level.

Helen takes me to the canteen and the buzz of conversation is so loud I struggle to hear her speak. We gather trays of food and she swipes what looks like an expense account and says over her shoulder, "I've ordered you one of these. They come with the package. It shouldn't take long, but keep any checks and I'll make sure you get the money back." I'm silent because I didn't expect this. Thinking of my usual lunch that involved scraping together enough to buy the cheapest meal on a junior reporter's wages, when those who had made the grade already dined out on expense accounts, makes me doubt I should be here even more.

I follow her to a table in the corner of the room and she smiles as she sets her tray down.

"Normally I eat at my desk, this is a luxury."

Looking around at the general chaos, I wonder if I heard her right. "A luxury?"

She nods. "I forget other people exist most of the time. Much of my day is spent on my own, working in an office that has little sound. I kind of love the madness here. It reminds me that life goes on and there are actual humans working here."

"Unlike Mr. Prince, of course, I doubt that man's human."

She looks a little surprised and I check myself because gossiping about the main man is probably not wise, so I change direction and say with interest, "Have you worked for him long?"

"Three years, give or take a few months."

"Do you like it?"

I'm curious because I'd be bored if I had to work on my own all day. "Yes, I love it. It's interesting stuff and Mr. Prince, Dexter, is a good boss. Like most clever men though, he can be difficult, but only because he is always a thousand steps ahead of me and is waiting impatiently for me to catch up."

I wonder what relationship they have shared in the past because her eyes have glossed over a little and she appears lost in a pleasant memory and I hate the jealous surge that puts me off my food.

She looks at me curiously. "So, Holly, tell me how you came by this great opportunity? I mean, Dexter isn't one to dish out favors. I must say I'm impressed."

Now I feel like the complete imposter I am and shrug. "He liked an article I wrote, and we got talking. I mentioned this was my dream and I suppose he took me on as his charity project for the year."

"I doubt it. Dexter may be generous, but he would never give anyone a helping hand out of kindness. He must see something in you, Holly. You should be proud of yourself."

Once again, I feel uncomfortable because if she knew the real story, she wouldn't be so impressed then and I feel ashamed of myself and I suppose decide in a heartbeat that I will work my ass off to prove to myself mainly that I deserve this chance.

"Hey, Helen, long time no see."

I look up and see a good-looking man holding his tray of food and notice how Helen blushes as she smiles up at him. She likes him. It's so obvious a blind man could feel the vibes and he appears to feel the same because he can't tear his eyes away from her.

After an awkward silence, she says quickly, "Why don't you join us?"

He needs no second invitation and jumps beside her and she says with a catch to her voice, "Um, Steven, this is Holly, Dexter's new apprentice."

He looks at me in surprise and I smile nervously, "Um, hi."

"Apprentice. Wow, how did you grab that opportunity? You're one lucky lady."

His eyes travel my body, leaving me in no doubt what he thinks was part of the interview process and it makes me angry. Of course he thinks that, why wouldn't he because it's the truth? Dexter gave me this job because it was the perfect way to control me. To keep his little fuck toy close in return for the information he badly needed. There is no way in hell I would be here if it wasn't for that and every person here knows it.

I tune out and listen to them make small talk and stare at my lunch with a growing nausea. I have so much to prove to just about everyone, and I always have.

After lunch, Helen takes me to another part of the building and explains as we walk. "This will be your first assignment. Dexter told me to put you on the team running the Powers' story. Apparently, you 're familiar with this one already and have begun your research. He wants you to learn from the best and Mack Evans *is* the best, so word of advice, just listen and suck up his bastard ways because, despite being the creepiest guy around, he's the best at what he does."

Thinking of the story I was working on, I'm surprised to learn he already had a whole fucking team doing what he asked me to do in an evening. She must notice my surprise because she says kindly, "You'll be fine. They're career driven people who love what they do. Learn from them and prove to them why you have the right to be there."

I look at her sharply because I wasn't aware I was giving off the doubt vibes, and she smiles. "Dexter told me you would struggle with imposter syndrome. It's normal, so don't think twice about it. When I got this job, I was working at the typing pool and applied, anyway. Everyone told me I had no chance of leapfrogging to the top job, so I went all out to impress. For a while there, everyone thought I'd slept my way into the position and never once thought I'd got here on my own merit. I've spent the entire three years proving I deserve the role, so if anyone knows what it's like to catch a break, it's me. Dexter sees things in people nobody else can, which is why he's so good at running this place. He puts the right person in the right job and that person is you, Holly. Now, I'm afraid I'll have to love you and leave you because I need to catch up with Dexter after his absence, but anything you need, the numbers in this phone or text or email me, anytime."

She hands me a phone and I look at it in surprise. "What's this?"

"Your phone. Your laptop is waiting at your desk and there's a folder waiting in your inbox with everything you need to know. Set it up and any problems, email me. Or run them through me at our weekly meetings."

"Weekly?"

"Yes, didn't Dexter explain? You work in this department for three months before moving to another. Learn the business from the inside and then move to the next lesson. I am your point of contact and if you have any questions, I will try to answer them and what I can't, I'll put on my list to ask Dexter."

"I won't get to ask him myself?"

"No, Holly, Dexter will not be involved in your training. I thought you already knew that?"

Feeling like a boat cast adrift in a turbulent sea, I try to smile bravely. "Yes, of course, silly me."

Yes, silly me indeed, because now I understand perfectly. He may have arranged this opportunity, but wants nothing to do with me outside of our other arrangement. Well, that's fine by me because I intend on throwing myself into work and who cares how I got the job, anyway?

All that matters is that I'm here now.

～

I HATE Mack Evans on sight. As soon as Helen introduces us, she disappears off, leaving me with a total misogynist. He barely gives me a backward glance as he snaps, "Ah, the new recruit. I can see why Dexter chose you. Your assets are notable."

I actually can't believe he just said that as he stares at my chest and then says dismissively, "Mine's strong and black. The kettles inside the third door on the right. Ask the others what they want and then I'll get one of them to talk you through what we do."

I know better than to argue because obviously I'm the least important person here and with a sigh, head off to resume my position as the one person in the office who is disposable and needs to perfect her coffee making skills before her journalistic ones.

By the time I've made just about everyone here a coffee, a woman with a bored expression stops by and says blankly, "I'm Joanne, Mack's asked me to walk you through things."

"Hi, I'm…"

"Anyway, here's your desk." She points to a desk on the edge of the office near the restroom and I see a laptop and nothing else in a cubicle the size of me. "It's not much, but all you need is space to type, anyway."

She looks bored as she says, "Every evening you'll get an email with your duties for the next day. Mainly research, with the odd meeting thrown in. Dress to impress at all times because honey, as a woman in a man's world, I can tell you those men don't see past your tits and if they like what they see, you last a bit longer."

"Seriously." I feel angry already, and she rolls her eyes. "You get used to it. Just play the bastards at their own game and prove that you're better than them. They'll soon learn. It's probably also best if you don't fuck any of them. The last girl that did thought it would help her career. It didn't. She just became an embarrassment, a reminder of their own weakness and was reassigned to the local rag."

I feel sick as she studies her nails. "Be better, Holly, that's my advice. Be better than all of them and then they have no excuse to replace you."

Somebody calls her over and she sighs. "I should get back.

You know, us girls should stick together, so if there's anything you need, a sympathetic ear perhaps, you can always call on me."

She nods and heads off, leaving me alone and feeling way out of my depth. But I wanted this. This is what I betrayed my family for, so I should suck it up and run with it to make it count.

CHAPTER 41

DEXTER

*J*t's been a long day. After Ryder's visit, I spent the rest of the day preparing to leave again. Catching up on emails, meetings and signing off stories makes the hours shoot past and I don't give Holly a thought until the moon shines outside my window and I notice it's seven already.

Feeling bad that I've left her on her first day, I check my phone to see where she is. I doubt she knows about the tracking device I activated on her phone and smirk to myself. Yes, I may have set my baby free, but she will always be under my control.

Noting that she's not even in the office, I feel the irritation pushing against my reasoning when I see she's at the bar across the street. I'm guessing she went with the rest of the hacks to the usual after work binge and just thinking of her with those bastards makes me so angry, I'm liable to do something I regret. Instead, I just fire off a quick text.

My office now.

She doesn't reply and I tap my fingers on the desk angrily when five minutes pass.

Typing again, I put in capitals. ***NOW!***

Trying to turn my attention back to business, I find it impossible as I imagine her being hit on by every bastard in that team and it's only when the phone vibrates, I look down and see her reply.

Sorry, my BOSS invited me out for a drink to get to know me better.

Seriously, that fucker had better not be getting any ideas about my new apprentice.

Beating out a response, I type.

I don't fucking care. Make your excuses and meet me in my office. We're going home, unless you want to fuck him for a bed for the night.

I watch with some satisfaction five minutes later, the little dot on my screen moving toward the building. I knew this was a good idea. I can keep tabs on her and she doesn't even know.

It takes her around twenty minutes to navigate the security and make her way to my office and as the door opens, I look at her with a sense of pride. There she is, my woman.

She looks weary, as if she's just worked for a week, and I note the tired eyes that are staring at me apologetically.

"I'm sorry, sir. I didn't think I could refuse. I need to bond with the team, it's exhausting."

She sighs and I shrug. "Bond with them in another way through the work you do, not the drinks you consume before they try to fuck you a welcome."

She looks shocked and I shrug. "You think I don't know what goes on? Those men are animals, aren't we all in fact, which is why I am eager to take you home—to bed."

"Home?"

I grab my briefcase and smirk. "Yes, home, Holly, because now you have another role to fulfill and I need to show you your office."

I head out of the room and ignore the pained look in her eyes as I expect her to follow me like a geisha girl. Tonight,

Holly will learn just what she signed up for and after the day I've had, I'm impatient to distance my mind from the impending nightmare that just won't go away.

Sam is waiting as we hit the lobby and falls into step beside me.

"It's all set, everything's in place."

"Good."

Holly is running to keep up and I wonder how she'll react when she learns I moved her apartment to mine and canceled her rental. She'll be pissed no doubt, but surely my penthouse is a welcome swap. Her one bedroomed apartment on the rough side of town must be a welcome sight in her rear-view mirror out of there.

My car is waiting and Sam holds open the door and I step inside, closely followed by Holly and as Sam jumps into the front, I remove the papers from my briefcase and set about using the time I have before we arrive.

Holly is silent and I forget she's here until she coughs nervously, "Um, thanks for the heads up about the Powers story. It really helped to know the backstory when I arrived. It didn't make me sound like an idiot when they were discussing it."

"You're welcome."

I carry on reading and she laughs nervously, "It's been a strange day."

Placing the documents back in the case, I sigh. "Holly, as much as I love knowing you enjoyed your first day, it doesn't run my empire, so word of advice, when I'm working, shut the fuck up."

She looks as if I've slapped her and I feel bad about that, but the last thing I need is banal conversation when I have so much to do.

She stares angrily out of the window and I carry on with

my reading and as the time ticks by, I sense an ever-growing distance forming between us and know she's pissed.

Sighing, I replace the contents and say wearily, "I'm sorry, baby, it's been a fucking exhausting day and the reason I want to get this out of the way is because I want to spend the rest of the evening inside you."

She still says nothing and I hate the frosty atmosphere that's developed inside the car and say with a sigh, "Look at me, Holly."

She turns and the daggers in her eyes make me smile because I love the fire in her I am doing my best to put out and reaching out, I pull her toward me and grind my lips onto hers. At first, she is stiff and unyielding and then as I slide my hand up her skirt and feel the soft skin trailing up to her thigh, I love the soft moan she gives as I find my way to her already drenched pussy.

Pushing her panties aside, I play with her clit until she gasps and then as I enter two fingers inside her opening, she grinds down on them as I pump hard. Biting her lip, I relish the small scream that I capture in my mouth and as she comes hard on my fingers, I whisper, "Better."

She nods and almost immediately the angry look has been replaced by a happier one and I say gently, "We both have some adjusting to do and I have never shared this ride home with anyone before. I'll meet you halfway though because I want you to like living with me, despite what you think."

Licking my two fingers, one by one, I see the lust re-enter her eyes and I grin.

"First, we eat and then we fuck. Welcome to your new home, baby."

"About that." She seems uncertain and I nod. "Yes."

"I already have a home. I should really go and check on it."

"It's gone."

"What do you mean, gone?"

"I had your stuff moved to mine."

"Seriously?"

"You're welcome."

"I wasn't thanking you. Why would you do that, it's my home, you had no right?"

"I had every right, Holly, because under the terms of our contract, you now belong to me."

"Belong to you, are you kidding me?"

"No, I'm not. You see, in the terms and conditions of the contract you signed, it clearly states that you will live with me and be at my disposal twenty-four hours a day. In return, I will pay all your expenses, and provide you with a home. You have one day off a week, unless you are granted more by prior arrangement and only if I agree. So, as I said before, welcome home, Holly, because you're mine now."

"You think." She is angry, and that excites me. "What if I want to renegotiate the terms of that so called contract, surely I have a cooling-off period?"

"Twenty-four hours and that expired already."

"You bastard."

"Thank you."

The car stops and as the door opens, she bolts from it like a gazelle from a lion and I watch her expression as she takes some deep breaths and stares around her in shock.

We are in my private underground car park and it is stuffed full of performance vehicles, all bearing my personal number plate.

Sam smirks as he steps aside to let me pass and I know he is loving every minute of this because he likes seeing me have to work for something for once.

As we step inside my elevator, Holly stands as far away from me as possible, and I sense an interesting evening ahead.

The tension is a major turn on for me and so as soon as we step foot inside the apartment and Sam heads off to his own wing of it, I drop my case and say roughly, "I think we need to set the rules in place, follow me."

I lead her to the impressive open space living room that wraps around the view of the city, and she stares in disbelief at the decadent paradise I have created. Soft cream carpeting, low comfortable seating and dim intimate lighting, all designed to offer the ultimate in relaxation. The only splash of color comes from the art on the walls, and the modern fireplace springs into life as the timer kicks in.

Pouring us both the ever-present whiskey, I nod toward the couch.

"Make yourself at home, baby, this is how things work around here."

Ripping off my tie, I know she is trying to look anywhere but at me and so I say firmly, "Look at me when I'm speaking to you."

She reluctantly drags her eyes to mine and I smile.

"Better. Now, Holly, during the day you work your ass off, proving to yourself and everyone around you why you wanted that job so badly. Make it count and suck up the shit they throw at you and learn. I expect nothing less of you and want you to learn the business so you can be the best. Then, we return here and you follow a different set of instructions. You agreed to be my submissive, to be controlled by me, and it's exactly what the word implies. I control you. We enjoy a mutually satisfactory relationship, but it's a business one and never forget that. I will treat you well and you will not want for a thing, but I must make it clear that emotion is not part of the deal. Do I make myself clear?"

"Yes, sir."

"Good. Now we must eat, you must be hungry, so I'll show you to your room where you will find your clothes waiting for you."

I reach out and take her hand and pull her up and then lead her to the part of the apartment she will call hers.

"In here is your bedroom, and the closet leads into the bathroom. If you need anything, charge it to my account. A card is on its way as we speak. I expect you to be available to me when I call and you get one day off a week. But there will be no other men. No dates after work, despite how innocent they make them sound. No friends over and no hobbies. You will be contactable at all times and I expect you to honor your agreement. You will sleep here at night and only when I have finished with you."

I look around the room and congratulate my designer on making it look pretty. Unlike my own room, this one is feminine, with its white drapes and bedding and pretty pink cushions. A woman's wet dream in every way and I know Holly will come to love it here.

Turning my attention back to her, I say happily, "You will have the use of my driver to go shopping if you need anything and I will assign you protection to keep you safe."

"Protection?" She looks confused, and I shrug. "There are a lot of mad bastards out there, Holly, who want to make a name for themselves. Being with me makes you a target. I'm sorry. What can I say, shit happens."

Walking into her closet, I reach for a black strapless silk dress and smile. "Wear this to dinner with no underwear and those black heels you love so much. You have thirty minutes."

Without a backward glance, I leave her to do as I say and congratulate myself on the perfect arrangement for us both.

CHAPTER 42

HOLLY

I hate him. I actually think I hate Dexter fucking Prince right now. He wasn't kidding when he said things would be different here. This is one big, sick joke, it must be.

As I look around, I stare at a room that makes me want to hurl. It's all white and pink like a candy cane and he has got this so wrong. I'm not that girl. The one who bats her lashes as he showers her with material possessions. I like my lines edgy and bold. Modern sleek lines and powerful colors. Not this shout out to Barbie. What a fucking joke.

Then there's this whole fuck toy job he tricked me into. I actually have no say in my life because he has chained me to his side by giving me what I foolishly asked for. Every fucking thing.

Him, the job, the opportunity, but in snatching it like the greedy bitch I am means I have sacrificed my integrity.

Sex is the driving force behind that because I want him— all the time it seems, but I want the Dexter from the picnic. My sexy cowboy with the gentler side. The man who showed emotion and made me feel like a queen, not the cold, unfeeling bastard, who makes me feel like the whore I apparently am.

Spying the black dress, I wrinkle my nose in disgust. He's even dressing me now to play out some sick fantasy he's been obviously planning for some time.

Then there's my apartment. What the actual fuck. I have nowhere to go, he's seen to that too and even if I go shopping, it's with him keeping tabs on me. I may as well be back in that cow prison for all the freedom I have, and as the full horror of my situation hits, I feel like the most foolish bitch alive. I sold myself and there is no escaping from that.

It's been a long day and it appears will be a long evening and so with resignation, I head to the shower to cleanse away my bad mood. I can do this. It's what I wanted. I asked for this. Maybe it's just all been too much and I'll think differently tomorrow.

By the time I follow instructions and meet him in that amazing room, I have adjusted my attitude and am just looking forward to eating. Why not take advantage of this situation myself? I get the best of everything after all, and my own space to sleep in at night. Maybe this is the way forward, women choosing to use men like Dexter like he's using me. I'll use him for sex and position and it will be on my terms—mentally anyway, he still has control, but I'll work on that.

The sight that greets me strengthens my resolve because God help me, this man just looks at me and I orgasm.

As I head toward him, he casts that lazy look over my entire body and it heats me inside, imagining what will happen later. He has changed into sweatpants and a t-shirt, and casual Dexter is as mouth-watering as corporate Dexter but still not a patch on cowboy Dexter.

He pours me a glass of champagne and I raise my eyes. "Are we celebrating?"

"Of course, this is your new home, welcome."

Taking the glass, I sip the cool liquid and shrug. "It will do I suppose."

"Is that so." He seems mildly amused and I nod disparagingly. "Yes, I would have done it differently. Less bland, bolder, more modern, giving it some actual personality instead of the bland one that obviously reflects the brief you gave your interior designer."

"Then change it, I don't care."

"I won't have time."

"Probably not."

He seems to be enjoying himself and looks interested. "So, how are you feeling about things now you've had time to settle in?"

"Fine I guess. I'll just make the best of a bad situation and use you for sex like you intend on using me."

I maintain an indifferent expression, and he grins, his eyes flashing wickedly. "Is that so? How will you use me, this I'd like to hear?"

"I don't know." I shrug. "I suppose just let you orgasm me out of boredom because being a kept woman wasn't really high up on my agenda in life."

"You want your own empire, of course, I remember."

"Good, then it won't come as a shock to you when I achieve what I set out to do and quit this freaky setup altogether."

He sets down his glass and waves toward the couch. "Tell me what you want, really want and I'll see if I can help out with that."

"No thanks, I'll figure it out on my own. Anyway, did you say we were going to eat first? I'm starving and would rather get this over with so I can get an early night."

He looks angry–finally, and I hope he feels as cheap as I did when he made me feel like a whore.

"We'll eat."

He nods toward the door and I follow him to a dining room

that takes my breath away. Once again, the room is floor to ceiling windows and even has a glass floor that is suspended over a fish tank containing beautiful exotic fish that swim gracefully beneath our feet. The candles that flicker on the glass table and glass side tables create a seductive warm atmosphere and the soft music plays from hidden speakers and I blink in amazement at the opulence this room brings.

The table is set for an intimate meal for two and what appears to be shrimp cocktail waiting for us. He holds out a chair and says pleasantly, "Your table awaits."

As I cross the room, I smile. "It appears you can even walk on water; I'm impressed."

"You'd better believe it."

As he pushes in my chair, he places a napkin on my lap and dusts my neck with his lips and a delicious shiver passes through me.

Trying so hard not to give him the reaction he wants, I lift my glass and take a swig, looking out across the skyline as he takes his seat opposite.

He starts to eat and I say in awe, "You have a lovely home, sir, or am I allowed to call you Dexter?"

"What do you want to call me?"

"Something else." I grin and he laughs softly.

"I'm guessing I wouldn't like it, so we'll stick with Dexter outside the bedroom and office."

Looking down, I realize I have no cutlery and as I look up, his wicked grin tells me it was no mistake, so I cock my head and shrug.

Spearing one of my prawns with his fork, he holds it against my lips and says huskily, "Eat."

"You're going to feed me. Why?"

"You'll see."

As my lips close around the fork, he says darkly, "Eyes on mine."

As I chew, I stare into his eyes and almost drown with lust at the expression in them. Every movement I make seems to be turning him on, and I'm enjoying the power I appear to have over him.

He feeds himself and then me, and it becomes a delicious game in more ways than one.

I wonder if the main course will suddenly materialize like a feast at Hogwarts with the owls bringing it in and dropping it before us, so I'm surprised when the door opens and a uniformed waiter heads into the room and says reverently, "Allow me."

He clears away the dishes and, as he works away, Dexter keeps my eyes fixed firmly on his with an unspoken command. By the time the waiter leaves the room, he has left a plate of what appears to be Lobster Thermidor and, once again, no cutlery for me.

Dexter feeds me slowly, and every mouthful is like a sex act. I actually squirm on my seat as I desperately try to remain indifferent, but by the end of the meal, we have spoken no words and just enjoyed a build-up of tension that will only end in one thing.

The music plays as the waiter returns and follows the same pattern and by the time he leaves, I've almost forgotten he was here at all because the whole time I have been concentrating on the man whose sole aim in life appears to be controlling me. It appears I can't even look at anyone but him when he commands it and, far from feeling angry about that, it feels so sexy I can't even breathe properly anymore.

He surprises me by saying, "Come here, Holly, and kneel at my feet."

I don't even question him, which shows what an idiot I am because not one hour ago I was answering back and proving how strong and independent I was. Now it all looks like a petulant childish act, as without hesitation, I kneel before him and he says gruffly, "Remove your dress."

Looking out at the bright lights of the city, I wonder if someone has their binoculars trained on me right now, but something about the edge to his voice tells me not to raise any doubts.

So, I hold his eyes and remove my dress and as it falls to the fish tank floor, I feel like the little mermaid sitting on a rock.

"Lie back I want to see all of you.

This is the weirdest experience of my life—actually probably not after the cow prison incident, but I do as he says and it feels as if I'm in a blue lagoon.

He drops beside me and empties his dessert on my body and I become some super-sundae as the ice cream burns my body and the cream and sauce trickle down my breasts. He removes his top and my pupils dilate because that view will never get old and as he leans down and licks and bites the food from my body, I shiver with delight and a euphoria it appears that only sex can give me these days.

He takes his time and as soon as he's finished, he stands and drops the sweat pants, leaving me under no illusion of what's going to happen next. Then he says lustfully, "On all fours."

Spinning around, I do as he says and as my own dessert hits the deck in a heap before me, he growls, "Lap it up."

"What the…" He grabs my hair and pulls my head back sharply and hisses, "Your punishment for talking back to me, baby. I told you I control you and I won't let you speak to me disrespectfully.

He pushes my face down toward the dessert and says, "Every last drop, lick the floor clean."

Once again, I feel humiliated as he stands behind me watching me lap at the floor like a dog and as my ass moves higher for me to reach the food, he grabs my hips and slams into me from behind and I almost choke at the force of it. "Keep lapping."

He thrusts inside as I eat from the floor and for some reason, this whole sick pleasure turns me on. The fact my ass is so high brings him in at a weird angle and it only stretches me further as I try to concentrate on two things at a time.

I lick, he thrusts and when he pulls out with no warning, I almost howl in desperation. Spinning me around, he holds my hands above my head and slams into me from the front and I love the crazed look in his eye as he 'punishes' me.

As punishments go, I'm loving this one because I have never been so turned on in my life. The whole set up is weird and edgy and I lose myself in a delicious fantasy as he fucks me insatiably.

I feel the pressure build and my breath hitches, but before I come, he pulls out suddenly and shoots his seed all over my chest. His roar turns me on even more as he hisses, "You will not come tonight."

Fighting back the disappointment that I'll have to finish what he started later when I'm alone once again, he reads my mind and says, "You will stay with me tonight, so don't get any ideas about pleasuring yourself, it's not going to happen."

"But I thought you didn't sleep with anyone, what's changed?"

I sound breathless and slightly hysterical and he shrugs. "I changed my mind."

Really, is this man for real?

Stroking my face, he looks deep into my eyes and says softly, "I'm enjoying you too much to leave you alone because tomorrow I won't be here."

"Where are you going?"

It hasn't escaped my attention that we are still naked, suspended over a fish tank and the floor could use some serious disinfectant right now, but he's leaving. Where?

"I have urgent business to attend to and will be away for one week. You will have full use of my driver, but I expect you to use the time wisely and work hard and rest for my return."

"Can't I just go back to my apartment?"

"I told you, you don't have one anymore. This is your home now."

"Well, visit my parents then, they must be worried."

I actually feel bad this is the first time I've thought of them and he shakes his head. "They're not home."

"Where are they then?" Images of them on a road trip to find me, with missing posters nailed on every wooden surface, spring to mind and he scares me by looking upset, which instantly causes me anxiety.

"Your father went back to his unit and your mom is on vacation in the South of France."

"What did you say?"

Pushing him away, I sit up and stare at nothing as I try to make sense of what he just told me.

"I'm sorry, Holly." He rubs my back as I whisper, "They don't care and they never have."

A lone tear escapes as I face my life head on and don't like what it's telling me. I actually have no one. The only person that wants me is this dominant man who just wants to fuck me. He just wants my body, not me—Holly Bryant. I have nobody and it's like the slap in the face I badly need right now because it tells me that the only person I can genuinely count on in life, is the woman who just sold herself to the devil, which tells me how fucked up I really am because she obviously can't be trusted either.

CHAPTER 43

DEXTER

I spent the rest of the night holding Holly and trying to make her relax and feel better about things. I couldn't back down on my word though, and that came back to bite when all I wanted was to have sex with her all night. Somehow that moment passed because I could tell how upset she was and just needed someone to hold, which is why I'm so irritable today.

I left before she even woke up and hated myself for that, but she looked like a sleeping angel and after the shock of yesterday, I thought she could use some sleep.

Maybe a few days away from me is what she needs to come to terms with her situation.

My helicopter is waiting to deliver me to the private airfield where my jet is waiting and as the chopper lifts off, I strangely wish she was bedside me. But I must do this alone. Sam and my security team are my only companions on a trip that could change everything.

Thinking about how she will cope when I'm gone worries me a little. I never even asked how she felt about the team I assigned her to, making her feel as if I didn't give a fuck. I do, more that I'm comfortable with and so I count this trip as a blessing in disguise for both of us because it's been too much too soon already and I need to re-focus my mind on how I want this arrangement to work.

The private plane is waiting and I can already see my luggage being loaded, along with the rest of my team.

I know the other Kings will be making a similar trip and wonder what they're thinking now. Like me, I'm sure they're worried because we are not in control of this situation and just thinking of who is sets my teeth on edge.

The King.

The man in charge, although a different one to our usual colleague.

Things have already changed, and we thought was just a continuation of the old school. It appears this King has written a different business plan and I'm not sure we're required.

As the plane takes off and I nurse a whiskey opposite Sam, I hope things are resolved by the time we make the return journey.

The final King—royalty. The only one who wears that particular crown by birth right. The man in charge and the controller of all our destinies. American royalty, removed from the spotlight to live a secret life. Away from the crowds, specu-lation and adoration. Secretly ruling over us under the radar, controlling the government and life as we know it. Politicians come and go and our President changes every five to ten years but royalty stays. A constant in an ever-changing life. Choosing its own soldiers to fight for our country in a much more stable way. It's always worked well before, since the decision was made centuries ago and yet this could be the moment every-thing changes.

Why is he doing this and what is Ryder's plan to save us all because if our King wants to cut us dead on the spot, he can and there would be no recriminations?

~

SIX HOURS later and the sky changes outside. The blue sky turns gray and we fly into a storm. Ironic when that's exactly how it feels and as we plunge through the clouds, I take my first look at the island he calls home.

Andromeda

Ruler of men.

The central point of the crown with the four of us sitting on either side.

Our newest addition is Maxim Augustus, due to the fact his father died, and he inherited the title of King. I feel sad for Rex; he was a good man and will be missed by us all. But his son is an enigma, a loose cannon. What is his plan because if he is going to change everything, it won't go down well?

CHAPTER 44

HOLLY

*H*e left without saying goodbye. Not even a note and yet I just feel empty inside. What did I expect, anyway? True to his word, he did sleep with me but must have left somewhere in the early hours because I woke up with a cold space beside me and an outfit chosen by him that I must wear today.

Arrogant prick.

As I finger the soft material of the business suit he pulled out, I wonder what runs through that man's head. He likes to control at all times, but sometimes the softer side of him spills out. I like that side of him and wonder if over time he will change. Maybe he will grow to love me. Stranger things have happened and so I push aside any worries I have and head to work as instructed.

"Coffee, Holly."

As soon as I drop my purse on my desk, Mack appears and barks his instructions.

Sighing, I turn and head to the kitchen and note I'm not alone. One of the other members of the team is pouring water into a mug, and he looks me up and down as I step inside the room.

"Here she is, the chosen one."

He sneers, and it instantly gets my back up.

"Excuse me." Toby is one of the guys who gives me the creeps because he makes no secret of the fact he is constantly ogling my tits.

"What's the matter, can't you take a joke now, or is there something you don't want me to know, like what you had to do to get the job, perhaps?"

"I don't know what you mean."

I glare at him angrily and he smirks, edging a little closer. "It's ok, darlin', we all do what we must. Luckily for you, God gave you a pair of tits that would distract any man, and I'm guessing Dexter was no different. What's the deal, you suck his cock, and he rewards you with a job, classy."

The fact it's true means shit right now and I hiss, "Keep telling yourself that when I tread on you on my way up the ladder. You'll see why Mr. Prince hired me soon enough. Have you ever wondered if there's a different reason I'm here? Maybe you should think about that before you talk your way out the door."

The fact he loses every drop of color in his face gives me a moment's satisfaction and then he hisses, "What's the matter, too close to the truth for comfort? Watch yourself, Holly, because if you don't fuck your way to the top in this establishment, nobody remembers your name. Word of advice, put up, put out and put those principles of yours in the trash because that's the only way a woman like you will get noticed in this place."

"So, hard work and skill count for nothing. You're a dinosaur, Toby, which is why I'll take great pleasure in wiping you out of existence myself."

He has the cheek to laugh and grabs his drink. "You know, I

really like you, Holly. I like your attitude. Fancy a drink after work, wipe the slate clean?"

"No thanks."

I turn my back on him and he laughs as he leaves, saying casually, "If you change your mind, you know where I am. Later, baby."

I actually can't believe that man. What a weirdo. As the kettle boils, his words hit home and I realize every person here is probably thinking the same. I don't have the moral high ground either when I think back on last night, as Dexter fucked me from behind as I ate off his floor.

Suddenly, I'm weary, so weary and feeling quite sick, actually. This isn't what I thought it would feel like. I'm full of self-hatred, self-loathing and self-destruction. I have no one to turn to who has my best interests at heart and I have betrayed my own family to get here. My apartment is gone and the man who made it all happen has left for God only knows where, and I have no idea when he'll be back.

To cap it all, I'm expected to work with people who make me sick and think I'm just a ladder climbing whore and they are right. I hate myself and I hate what I've done, but there is absolutely nothing I can do about that.

He has broken me.

SOMEHOW, I make it through the day.

Mack has been vile toward me today and chewed my ass off on more than one occasion in front of the whole team. Then someone slapped that ass when I walked past and wouldn't own up. The rest of the guys all just sniggered like kids leaving me feeling humiliated once again. It appears I should get used to that.

When I return to the apartment, it feels empty. Too big for any normal person and emotionless, as if it has no heart.

Dexter doesn't even call, telling me he doesn't care about me either, and as the tears fall while I eat a solitary meal for one at the table in the dining room, I feel like the loneliest woman alive.

The next day is no different, or the next, and I wonder if this is what I can expect. To be treated like trash by just about every person in my life right now and so impulsively I decide to call Dexter just to hear his voice, but as soon as Helen answers it, my heart sinks.

"Hey, Holly, how can I help you?"

"I um, thought I was calling Dexter."

"You are, but he had his calls redirected to my phone. He's incommunicado as they say and even I can't reach him."

"What about Sam?"

"Is everything alright, honey, you can ask me anything?"

She breaks off and I hear her giggle and a man's voice say sleepily, "Who is it? Come back to bed."

She says quickly, "Um, sorry, Holly, this isn't a good time. I'll call you tomorrow, sleep well."

She cuts the call and I feel so frustrated, I toss the phone across the room in a fit of rage.

Regretting that almost immediately, I run after it and catch my foot on the table and fall to the ground with a squeal. The pain shoots through my ankle as I curse, and the tears fall when I realize I've probably sprained it.

In the end, I just lie where I am and wait for the pain to subside and the tears that are never far away fall as I realize all of my options have gone. This is it - my life.

By the time I drag myself to bed, my foot is throbbing, my head hurts and I feel sick and despite having been served an amazing meal by the silent waiter, I couldn't eat a thing because my appetite appears to be a thing of the past.

The only thing left to do is to retreat to my bed, but the sight of the princess palace makes me feel even more nauseous, so I raise my middle finger to it and head toward what I think is Dexter's room.

As soon as I step inside, I know I was right. It reeks of him. The scent of a man who even now is sending me delirious with lust. Just the smell of him that lingers is turning me on, so I head to the bed and strip off all my clothes, loving how good the silk sheets feel against my skin.

This room is like Dexter, masculine, raw and so sexy it offers an instant orgasm.

Picturing the man himself, I play with myself, imagining his mouth where my fingers are and as I bring myself to a climax, I burst into tears.

I hate myself so much and yet what the hell do I do now?

WHEN I WAKE the next day, I'm wrapped in Dexter's sheets after having dreamed all night about the man himself. He is so inside my head it's not even funny and as my eyes open, I feel the waves of nausea wake up with me.

I just about make it to the bathroom before I hurl into the basin and as I collapse trembling to the floor, a horrible thought occurs to me.

I'm pregnant.

The more I try to reassure myself I'm not, the more something tells me I am. Quickly, I think back over the past couple of weeks. I can't be. I'm on the pill for Christ's sake. Of course I'm protected.

My head is now hurting and the thought of having to deal with this too is driving me insane and once again the truth hits me like a slap in the face. I have no one to turn to.

Dexter would be mad, probably throw me out, or kill me even. I wouldn't put that past him.

Maybe I'm wrong, I must be. I'll take a test, grab one in my break from the CVS in the street outside. Nobody will ever know. *I'll know.* It's probably a false alarm anyway and just that lobster from the other day. Maybe Dexter has it too and is a sick as a dog. I kind of hope that's the case.

Feeling a little more able, I quickly shower and change and head off to meet the driver, who smiles at me courteously. "Good morning, Holly."

"Morning, Jenkins."

As I step into the car, I say foolishly, "Um, please can you stop at the drug store, I need a few things."

He nods. "Of course."

Luckily, he chooses one a short distance away and I don't need to worry that anyone sees and I am soon armed with a pregnancy test. In fact, four of them and some other supplies I need.

As soon as I head to the office, I make my first stop the restroom and as I pee on the stick, I keep everything crossed because God help me if I'm right.

A few minutes later and the evidence punches me straight in the face.

I was right.

I feel sick again but for a different reason his time.

It's positive. I'm pregnant with Dexter Prince's baby and he will think I planned it. To trick him, entrap him, and make him love me. How has this happened? Whoever manufactures that contraceptive pill needs to know immediately. I should sue, clean them out because I will need every penny now because there's only one thing for it—I have to run.

CHAPTER 45

DEXTER

ONE WEEK LATER

*S*omehow, we made it back, but I'm not sure I will ever shake the memory of what happened. The journey home is a silent one, as we all deal with it in our own way.

I'm pretty certain I'm not the only one who was shocked beyond belief by a wedding I will never forget and as I make my silent journey home, all I can think of is Holly.

I wanted to call her so many times, but phones are banned on Andromeda for a very good reason.

Now it's the most important thing in my life right now to hold her in my arms and make it better.

As soon as we land, I take out my phone and turn it on for the first time in a week and, as expected, the messages take some time to come through.

I can't begin to deal with them now and immediately look for the tracker to locate the only person I want to see right now and am happy to see she's right where I left her.

The journey is short but still too long as I make my way to a woman who has surprised me. I want her. I think I even love her because for the first time since I lost my sister, I can see a future with someone. Holly. The woman I kidnapped, imprisoned, and made my slave. Now the tables have turned and none of that means shit anymore. I want a wife and I want it to be her.

I almost run into the apartment and call her name, hoping like crazy she's not asleep already. I'm tired, emotional and weary and, for a man who likes to be in control, I'm losing it fast.

Opening every door in my penthouse, I am greeted with empty rooms and it doesn't even look as if she's slept here at all.

It's only when I find the phone I gave her neatly stacked with the laptop and credit card, the penny drops. She's gone. There isn't even a note and there is not one trace left of the woman I have finally realized means more to me than anything.

Quickly, I call Sam.

"Holly's gone, find her."

"Have you checked her phone?"

"I'm not an idiot."

"Just checking."

He cuts the call and I feel the frustration tearing me up inside. She left. I can't believe she actually did it. She left me.

I suppose, along with the shock of the past few days, this one hits me even harder. I was so certain she would be waiting for me. Welcome me home with open arms and happy tears as I pledge my undying love for her. That's how messed up I am because this week has been an epiphany for me and I can't believe she's not here to share it.

I can't concentrate on anything but her and completely ignore the messages that keep coming through. I check them in case its news of Holly, but angrily discard them if they're not.

Sam calls and I seize the phone eagerly. "Have you found her?"

"The choppers on its way."

Quickly, I race to the roof and see Sam already waiting and as the helicopter comes in to land, I wonder where she is. Media Corp perhaps, working to prove herself, I wouldn't put it past her, but as we buckle up, Sam instructs the pilot to head for the Ranch.

On the way, he fills me in on what he knows and I just stare at him in horror as he shakes his head, looking worried.

I can't even speak. I'm so shocked and yet I can only think of one thing I want right now and it's feeling her in my arms.

Sam interrupts and says sympathetically, "Maisy left me a message to call her. I didn't think it was urgent, so I parked it. I'm sorry."

Scrolling through my own messages, I see several from her and Jason too and my heart sinks. Why am I such an idiot?

I open the first one and see the words dance before my eyes.

As soon as you land, make for the ranch.

She's in a bad way, hurry.

Sorry, Dexter, she'll be so angry I told you where she is, but you have to come—now.

Jason's are much along the same lines and the worried look on Sam's face is nowhere near as bad as I feel inside.

Poor Holly. Why did I treat her so badly?

As soon as we land, Jason is on hand with the jeep and from the look on his face, he's worried, which doesn't make me feel any better.

As we head off, he shouts, "I've saddled your horse, you can change at the stables."

Glad of his help, I quickly change into my jeans and plaid shirt and grabbing my hat take Saracen's reins, who also seems to feel the urgency of the situation.

Without a backward glance, I ride like fury because every minute I'm away from Holly is one she doesn't know I love her. As I even *think* the word, it surprises me I've come this far and the only person who needs to hear it is Holly herself.

By the time I lead Saracen into the clearing, I have run through every possible thing I'm about to say in my mind.

When I see her on the edge of the water, Summer tethered nearby, my heart physically thumps in my chest as I watch her beaten form throwing stones into the lake, looking so broken I feel like the biggest bastard alive.

She looks up as I approach and the blood drains from her face and the tears spill down her face as she whispers, "I'm sorry."

CHAPTER 46

HOLLY

*H*e's here. I can't believe he is, but just seeing him standing beside his horse undoes me in a way I never thought it would.

I feel like such a failure. I had nowhere to go, and this is the only place I could think of. It took me some time to plan my journey because I couldn't trust Dexter's driver not to phone him. So, I hired a car and turned up late one night. Maisy welcomed me in like I knew she would, and I have spent the past few days trying to come to terms with how things have turned out.

I know they've been worried about me. I've seen the looks they share and expected they would tell their boss I was here. They work for him after all and, as his friends, their loyalty lies with him. But I had nowhere else to go, because all I wanted was to spend some time thinking about what happens next.

Now he's here, watching me with a strange expression on his face, and I know he knows. He's probably so angry and rightly so. I'm pregnant when I told him I was protected. I would be too in his situation.

To my surprise, he walks toward me with a gentle look on his face and says sweetly, "You scared the hell out of me."

"I'm sorry." It's all I can think of to say and as he reaches me, he pulls me close and just holds me tightly. "Never leave me again, Holly, I can't deal with it."

I fall silent because leaving him is a joke when I ran to his other house. Hardly the great escape and as he rubs my back, he whispers, "I know about the baby."

Immediately, I stiffen up, waiting for the anger to show, but to my surprise he whispers, "Now it's my turn to be sorry. I left you to deal with this on your own. I failed you."

"You didn't know, neither of us did."

I pull back and look for any sign of anger in his expression, but all I see is emotion and that shocks me more than that pregnancy test result.

Dexter Prince is looking like he's going to cry and I stare at him in surprise as he whispers, "I love you, Holly. I think I did the moment you answered me back. I love your fire, your strength and the soft part of you that you struggle to hide. I love your ambition and your bravery and I'm the one who's sorry that I took so long to tell you."

"You love me... but how, when?"

I am so confused because I wasn't expecting this and he laughs softly. "I've had a really shit week, but don't ask me to tell you why because I can't even repeat what happened to myself. Just know it taught me a few things about myself that I didn't like."

He pulls me down beside him at the side of the lake and says in a tortured voice. "What I saw will live with me to my dying day and my only thought was of you. That if I never made it back, I would regret not telling you I loved you. Regret making your life so difficult and for being a bastard when I should have supported you. When I landed, I discovered you had to deal with shit all over again of my own creation. I'm sorry, Holly, and if you'll let me, I want to make it up to you for the rest of your life."

Turning, he looks at me and I am mesmerized at the emotion in his eyes because this man doesn't do emotion. He told me it wasn't an option, but that appears to have changed because the emotion in him that is hitting me hard right now is sparking hope inside me as he strokes my face and whispers, "Will you marry me, Holly?"

For the first time since I met him, Dexter looks anxious. Worried about my response and if there was ever a time I fell hopelessly in love with him, it's now at this special place as he stares deep into my eyes. I already know the answer is yes. I suppose I always hoped he would ask one day and whatever happened to him this week has done me a huge favor because it has accelerated our position at break neck speed.

Reaching out, I touch his face the same way and whisper, "Yes, Dexter, I will marry you."

Just for a moment, we stare, neither of us quite believing we've reached this point at all and then, as he kisses my fingers one by one, a huge smile breaks out across his face and he pulls me in and kisses me so hard I forget there was ever any doubt in my mind at all.

When he pulls back, I say almost fearfully, "I didn't mean to get pregnant. I'm sorry if you think I've trapped you."

He looks angry and my heart sinks, but then he shakes his head and smiles a huge shit-eating grin that makes me smile.

"I love that we're pregnant."

"We?" I laugh as he nods. "I can't wait to see my baby grow inside you. To know that we created a life and will be responsible for caring for a family. Just so you know, this is one of many. I'm thinking four, maybe five, what do you think?"

"Hold on a minute, I never agreed to five. Are you crazy?

"Crazy for you."

Laughing, he kisses me so deeply my toes curl and as the kiss deepens and he pushes me back onto the ground, he shows me just how happy he is, over and over again.

EPILOGUE

HOLLY

TWO YEARS LATER

$\mathcal{M}$aisy giggles as we watch a scene we never thought would be outside the window.

Dexter and Jason are deep in conversation, pushing two strollers toward the stables.

Maisy grins. "It suits them."

"I agree." I can't stop staring at the man I have fallen hopelessly in love with who I now call my husband.

Dexter arranged a wedding so quickly my head spun and we became Mr. and Mrs. Prince two months after he proposed.

It was a huge affair; the biggest society had seen for quite some time and I was overwhelmed at the number of guests and scale of decadence he arranged at such short notice. I just went along with it because I wanted him and would have been happy to marry him on a beach somewhere, or in town, because all that mattered was becoming his wife.

"How are you feeling, honey, you must be tired?"

Maisy smiles with concern and I sigh. "I'm fine most of the time, but this sickness never seems to go away."

I inadvertently rub my stomach that is now holding baby number three, and Maisy laughs. "Good job it's not twins again, you would definitely have your hands full then."

Laughing, I look out of the window at the two babies who surprised us so happily. One boy and one girl. Two gorgeous bundles of love that we both dote on. Phoebe and Jacob, two beautiful souls who Dexter is obsessed with and I laugh. "No, just one this time, it will be fine."

Maisy nods and looks at her own husband pushing her new-born baby.

"Fatherhood suits them."

"It sure does."

Sighing, I turn away from the window and groan.

"I've got this story to finish by close of business. I should get started if I'm going to reach the deadline."

"I'll fetch you a coffee and some apple cake. Go and do what you do, honey, and I'll do the same."

Smiling, I head off to my den that I share with Dexter and still can't quite believe how things worked out. Rather than go back to my apprenticeship, I now freelance for several of Dexter's channels of distribution. I've also got my own Vlog and have become quite the businesswoman since I put my mind to it.

As I settle down, I smile when I see the screensaver of our wedding photo.

Both sets of parents flank us on either side and for once my father looks proud. My stepmother was beside herself when she learned of my good fortune and has been bugging me ever since to become her new best friend. It always makes me laugh to see Colton standing awkwardly on the edge of the photograph, completely out of place and wishing he was anywhere but there. It turns out he helped Dexter with whatever problem he had and then ran off to join some biker gang.

We don't see much of him, but he shows up at family occasions and seems happy. I think he's also got a girlfriend because I heard him talking to Jason about some girl he was seeing, although the name appears to change every time he visits.

Looking at Dexter's parents, I smile happily because they look so proud of their son. It's still early days, but we are building bridges and he is relaxing more around them as he comes to terms with the guilt he's always felt after his sister's death. It's obvious they never blamed him for that, but he can't look them in the eye, but the kids have helped heal the rift a little and they visit often.

Sighing, I click on my laptop and set about having it all because Dexter encourages me to work and we both make sure that at least one of us is always here with the children. He flies in every evening from the city and sometimes Maisy and Jason babysit and we have date night at his penthouse. We may be equals outside the bedroom, but Dexter still loves to dominate inside it and I love every minute of it.

Yes, it's funny how things work out and our future is bright. Sometimes trust is all you need with a lot of love thrown in. The perfect recipe for marriage—at least I think so.

THANK you for reading Destroy a King, I really hope you liked it.

I'm sure you can't wait to find out what happened when Dexter met The King.

Read the prologue now.

MARRY A KING: THE GRADUATION BALL

The air is burning with anticipation and the graduates are hungry. It's all come down to this moment. So much is riding on this event and despite the excitement, there's a nervous energy that could make or break futures.

Graduation gowns have been replaced with silk and lace and mortar boards with tiaras. The scrubbed faces of childhood have been painted into adulthood as the rest of our lives beckon.

Nobody here underestimates the importance of this night, as life's tapestry has yet to be woven. Yesterday we bid goodbye to our childhood and today we welcome the future.

"You look beautiful, Calliope."

My mother's admiration settles my nerves a little as I look at myself critically in the mirror. As dresses go, nothing has been left to chance with this one and as I smooth down the glorious silk that stands stiff with pride over a gigantic hoop, I admire the deep red color she insisted on. Royal red it's called, which is exactly the purpose my mother has in mind.

She has no other desire than to see me marry and her sights are set on the King.

My sight is set slightly differently, but she doesn't need to know that.

As she fixes the family tiara in place, the pride in her eyes takes me back a little. "I am so happy for you, darling. You will make a beautiful bride."

"Hold on, mom, I've only just graduated. I'm not ready for marriage yet."

"Calliope!" Her lips thin in disapproval and the magic has gone in a puff of displeasure as she hisses, "Not this again, you must know your place."

"My place is at the Grosvenor School of Medicine. I thought we spoke about this."

"We did, and we agreed it's an honorable dream, but that's all it is. You will fulfill your destiny and marry. It was always going to be the way for you and no amount of dreaming will change your path."

I frown and she smoothes out the lines in my eyes with her fingers.

"Don't frown my darling, it makes you look ugly."

Looking at my mother's perfectly made-up face, crease free courtesy of her resident plastic surgeon, I feel the walls closing in on me. Cressida Brookes-Stanley is the model wife, model mom and model airhead and thank God I got my father's brains and not hers.

Loud footsteps approach and my mother licks her lips nervously, "It's time."

As the door opens, my smile is genuine, as the only man I have ever loved steps through the door. "Pa!"

I smile my welcome, and my mother frowns as he sweeps me into his arms and dips me to the floor. "My princess, how beautiful you look."

"William, do not mess up the goods. It's taken two hours to get her looking so perfect."

My heart sinks. The goods. That's all I am to my mother. A commodity to buy and sell and she shakes her head as she dusts an imaginary crease from my over-inflated skirt.

"We should go, the carriage awaits."

My heart sinks. Carriage. What century does this island live in?

As we make our way down the stone-clad corridor, I think about Andromeda. A world of its own, set apart from society, hidden from civilization to anybody who doesn't know of its existence. I've always wondered why they send their kids to school in places like England and America when all they want is for their daughters to marry well and their sons to end up as guardians of everything we hold dear.

I have never understood the importance of Andromeda as a society and always thought it a little backward really in its traditions. Take this ball, for example. They dress it up as a graduation ball, but we all know it's just a cattle market as the new adults shop for a husband or wife.

The carriage is waiting with the uniformed driver and my heart sinks. This is it. Destiny beckons and I wonder if my parents know I have another one in mind?

I've been well educated and excelled at that. Boarding school in England followed by Harvard university to study medicine. Secretly, I have applied for a place at a well-respected hospital as an intern and the letter arrived via email to a personal account I set up years ago. I can almost touch my freedom and tonight is just to humor my parents because I have a plan and it doesn't involve being married off anytime soon.

"You know this is your last chance to impress the King, Calliope and I'm counting on you to deliver. Everyone knows you are the most beautiful girl in Andromeda and expectations are high."

My mother drones on as my father checks his phone as usual because quite frankly this woman could bore a baby.

I remain silent because the last thing I want is to fight with her because this is her night, not mine. The moment when she can parade me around like a pet peacock and bask in the admiring glances of her friends as she proves to them that she won the lottery with me.

The approach to the castle is always an impressive one and as the carriage joins the line, it gives us enough time to watch with interest the impressive sight. Flaming torches burn as they guide our way along immaculate paths ablaze with flowers that appear almost too perfect. The washed stone of the castle looks almost jet washed and the impressive turrets make it feel like a fairy story.

It always feels a like a fairy story in Andromeda and it took living away from here to realize it's not real life. It counts for nothing, in my eyes anyway, because who wants to live in the pages of a fairy tale when the real world is so much more exciting?

"Now, Calliope, you must be on your best behavior, at your most demure and not entertain any of the childish ways you have developed a habit for. This is the moment you will have to work your hardest to secure the golden prize. Don't let me down because the whole family is counting on you. Your sister's own path will be determined by you because if you marry well, they will be guaranteed that same future."

I tune out as she drones on and think about what I left behind. Freedom. I was happy in England, and America made me fall in love for a very different reason. It was so exciting in Boston. So vibrant, full of life and where I loved the history and traditions of England, I adored the freedom of America. I made up my mind that is where I want to practice medicine and just thinking of the new life waiting for me fills me with excitement.

I have a plan, an escape one and tonight is my leaving ball because I have a ticket out of here and they will never be able to persuade me to give up on my dream.

We join the line of excited girls who are to proceed toward the ballroom like lambs to the slaughter on the arms of our parents. The high-spirited men are already safely inside, waiting and watching the sacrificial lambs to be presented to society. Taking their pick as we walk through the door and marking their cards, intent on plucking the best prize for themselves.

My mother is almost shaking with excitement as we make our way to the large double doors that appear centuries old and I see the liveried master of ceremonies announcing the names of every one who passes through them.

As we inch ever closer, the nerves join me and I wonder if I can really pull this off. Can I escape because it doesn't feel as if I can right now, so I plaster a blank look on my face as we take our turn.

The number fastened to my wrist tells the master what he needs to know and I hear him say in a booming voice, "Mr. and Mrs. Brookes-Stanley, present Calliope, Annalise, Brookes-Stanley."

As we step through the door into the great hall, the sea of faces watching us below makes me falter a little as the huge chandeliers hanging above almost blind me. I try anything possible to tune out and concentrate on not falling down the immense staircase that was obviously designed to crush a woman's dreams by way of a tripping hazard and I'm grateful for the strong hand of my father as he props me up as I glide down the stairs.

My mother is enjoying every second of this as she smiles and looks pompously around the room, knowing that she has the one many expect the king to choose. I almost daren't look in his direction because I want nothing to draw his attention to me and so I stare blankly ahead and try desperately to fade into the tapestries that line the room because I am hating every second of this.

Finally, we make our way to the edge of the crowd and I can breathe again as everyone's attention is diverted to the next girl in line and as I look around the room, I am desperate to find a friendly face because somewhere in this crowd are my three best friends enduring a similar journey.

Everywhere I look are beautiful gowns and elaborate masks because the men do not have the same rules as the women in Andromeda. Disguised by golden masks, their features are kept hidden as they feast their own eyes on the available women. Only when the last girl has paraded into the room do we get to wear our own masks, signifying that we are single and ready to play an important game. The number on our wrist reveals our identity, but under the rules of the evening, the only man who can lower our mask is the one who chooses us as his bride.

Get me out of here fast because this shit is so ancient it's almost funny and as the door closes with a resounding thud, I am so happy to remove my mask and place it firmly around my eyes. There. That's so much better.

"Now, Calliope, the hard work begins. I have located the King and will guide you over to where he is standing. It will be up to you to make a good impression if he looks your way, which I am certain of because he hasn't taken his eyes off you for a second since you stepped foot inside the room."

"Mother, please, of course he hasn't, you're just…"

"Enough Calliope, mother knows best. So come on, there is already an interested crowd around him and I will not let this moment pass."

"It's best to do as she says, princess, it always works for me." My father squeezes my hand gently and whispers, "She means well, don't ever doubt that."

"I know." I hang my head because I know she does. My mother only wants the best for us, and yet she can't understand that the best thing for me is to get the hell out of Andromeda.

Sucking it up, I do as I'm expected and allow her to parade me around the room, knowing that in just a few minutes I will be cast out on my own to bait a large fish and all I hope is to meet my friends and spend a good night gossiping together about how archaic this ball is.

Like me, my friends are so done with this place and have their own plans on leaving. Lauren wants to be a film director and is always making short films, usually involving the rest of us, and she's good. Some of them have won major prizes and I know she will be successful. Natalia wants to own her own company. She's a fashion designer and has made endless amazing dresses for us over the past few years when we had no money. Then there's Eloise who has fallen in love with her professor, but nobody needs to know that because the girls at this ball are expected to be virgins and most of them are, me included. But Eloise is a scandal waiting to happen and if I'm worried about anyone, it's her.

After parading the room for what feels like forever, mom does the decent thing and allows my father to guide her to the chaperone room, set a short distance away. Before they leave, she hisses, "Don't let me down, Calliope, we are counting on you."

My father pulls her away with a shake of his head, leaving me in glorious solitude so I can locate my friends.

Suddenly, a dark whisper comes from behind as a deep voice says, "What's a beautiful woman like you doing in a place like this?"

Resisting the urge to grin, I say icily, "Avoiding men like you."

Turning around, I smile at the man who is watching me with amusement shining through his mask. "Calliope, my darling, you look like a princess."

He mocks me and I roll my eyes. "You don't scrub up so bad yourself, Victor."

He mock bows and takes my arm and guides me over to the side of the room and if I could endure this evening on anyone's arm, it's his. Victor Augustus, the boy I sort of grew up with. Childhood friends and the one boy I can stand talking to for more than ten minutes. His only fault is his family because Victor Augustus is second in line to the throne.

"So, my darling, what happens now for Calliope Annalise Brookes- Stanley? Is this the moment we cement our union and put our parents out of their misery?"

"In your dreams, Victor."

He smiles, but I see an edge in his eye that takes me by surprise. "What's wrong?"

"I don't know." He sighs. "I suppose I'm finding this all quite difficult."

"I'm sorry, Vic."

I place my hand on his arm as he looks around the room wearily. "It's just that ever since our father died, things have been a little intense. Maxim is unbearable as usual and as the new King, everything is centered around him. He is impossible to be around because of what he's inherited and I'm just expected to suck it up and act the good second in command and help him navigate a sea of killer sharks."

"I'm sorry, Vic, maybe things will calm down when he chooses his wife and they sit on the throne of power together."

"Let's hope so. Anyway, what about you? I wasn't kidding when I said we could team up. It would be a sacrifice but I'd do it out of duty."

"You're good." I grin and sigh as I look around me. "I'm not interested in catching anyone's attention, if I'm honest. This whole scene grates on me."

He nods because out of anyone here, I think he understands the most. Like me, he was educated abroad and enjoyed a freedom many of us are finding hard to give back. Since childhood it has been drummed into us that our futures lie in Andromeda. The next generation. The next keepers of the faith, but how can we settle when we have seen what's out there?

"Anyway…" Victor's voice brings me back to the job at hand. "I'll fetch us a drink; I won't be long. If you want to escape the crowd and keep your virtue intact, I suggest you wait behind this tapestry. Nobody will see you there and it will keep those other horny bastards from taking what's mine."

"Thanks, but just for the record, Victor, I'm not yours, ok."

I grin as he rolls his eyes. "Keep telling yourself that, darling, we both know it's destiny."

He winks and heads off and I'm grateful about the heads up

and move through the giant tapestry onto a balcony that looks out across the Augustus Kingdom.

I feel a little sympathy for Victor because if I am expected to follow a certain path, his is far more guarded than mine and it's a lot to deal with.

The gentle breeze ruffles my skirt and I take deep, cleansing breaths of it. Allowing it to cast its comfort on my face as I struggle to get through this tedious evening.

A movement behind me makes me turn and I see Victor make his way onto the balcony. "Hey, where are the drinks?"

He appears empty handed and yet something is different about him. It's only when he comes closer that I realize its someone else entirely and I say slightly nervously, "Um, I'm sorry, but I should leave."

I make to pass him and a hand reaches out and grabs my wrist so hard it burns and pulls me toward him and as the other hand locks around my waist, I smell danger of the most intense kind.

The eyes that stare at me through the mask are the most intense ones I've ever seen. So dark, so deep, and so dangerous. They flash with a power that takes my breath away and holds my attention far longer than I'm happy with. There's such intensity in that look I am struggling to breathe and then he speaks with a voice that sounds like a thousand knives stabbing my heart in a frenzied attack.

"I've been waiting for you, Calliope."

"Who are you?" I really can't tell because the light is so dim and the shadow crosses his face.

"I'm your future."

I try to pull back because God forbid somebody actually removes my mask and chains me to his side forever, because how will I escape then? It's far too early in the evening for the unmasking ceremony and I intend on being long gone before that happens, so I say angrily, "Let me go, this is against protocol. You should know that."

He laughs as if the devil has entered the room and I almost think he has as he whispers darkly, "I choose you, Calliope and I don't need to wait for an unmasking ceremony for that."

"You do. Actually, it's in the rules. You must give everyone an equal chance and if you choose the same girl as another, it goes by order of nobility. Surely you know that."

He laughs and I wonder if he's slightly deranged because this laugh has no humor in it, just a wicked sense of fucked up.

He backs me against the railings and I briefly wonder if it could all end here this evening because the weight of us against it could have us crashing to the deep valley below.

Before I know what's happening, my mask is whipped from my face and tossed from the balcony and as I open my mouth to protest, his lips land on mine with a possession that seals my fate. He plunders, tastes and owns and as he pushes in hard, my huge dress does nothing to stop the feel of his body against mine and the fact he is devouring me in the moonlight. I have no room to move and almost can't breathe as he fists my hair and punishes my lips with a strength that takes my breath away.

As first kisses go, this is one that moves continents because despite how outraged I am, I'm loving every passionate moment of it.

A discreet cough behind us stops the attack, and it certainly felt like one and as he pulls away, I see the furious face of my friend glaring at us both, as he hisses, "What the fuck, her mask?"

My attacker steps away and says darkly, "Is at the bottom of the valley. Checkmate, Victor, I win."

I look between them in confusion as Victor looks as if he's about to toss this guy to go and collect it personally and then I watch in bewilderment as two uniformed guards' step onto the crowded balcony and say "Sire, the first dance, they are waiting."

Sire, what the fuck? I blink in surprise as he takes my arm and says in a dark voice, "Follow me."

"No!" I try to pull away and Victor says angrily, "Let her go, choose someone else."

This madman actually laughs. "We both know it was always her. Now stand aside and let us pass."

Victor looks so angry it completely changes him. There's an anger surrounding us that I can almost reach out and taste and as I'm pulled from the balcony beside a man who is scaring the hell out of me, my bright future may as well have joined the mask in the valley below because this man has cemented my future and I have no escape from that.

~

Carry on reading Marry a King

If you haven't caught up with the other books in the series check them out here.

Catch a King
Steal a King
Break a King
Destroy a King
Marry a King

Thank you for reading this story.
If you have enjoyed the fantasy world of this novel, please would you be so kind as to leave a review on Amazon?

Join my closed Facebook Group

Stella's Sexy Readers

Follow me on Instagram

CARRY on reading for more Reaper Romances, Mafia Romance & more.

Remember to grab your free copy of The Highest bidder by visiting stellaandrews.com.

ALSO BY STELLA ANDREWS

Twisted Reapers

Sealed With a Broken Kiss
Dirty Hero (Snake & Bonnie)
Daddy's Girls (Ryder & Ashton)
Twisted (Sam & Kitty)
The Billion Dollar baby (Tyler & Sydney)
Bodyguard (Jet & Lucy)
Flash (Flash & Jennifer)
Country Girl (Tyson & Sunny)

The Romanos
The Throne of Pain (Lucian & Riley)
The Throne of Hate (Dante & Isabella)
The Throne of Fear (Romeo & Ivy)
Lorenzo's story is in Broken Beauty

Beauty Series
Breaking Beauty (Sebastian & Angel) *
Owning Beauty (Tobias & Anastasia)
Broken Beauty (Maverick & Sophia) *
Completing Beauty – The series

Five Kings
Catch a King (Sawyer & Millie) *
Slade

Steal a King

Break a King

Destroy a King

Marry a King

Baron

Club Mafia

Club Mafia – The Contract

Club Mafia – The Boss

Club Mafia – The Angel

Club Mafia – The Savage

Club Mafia - The Beast

Club Mafia – The Demon

Standalone

The Highest Bidder (Logan & Samantha)

Rocked (Jax & Emily)

Brutally British

Deck the Boss

Reasons to sign up to my mailing list.

•A reminder that you can read my books FREE with Kindle Unlimited.

•Receive a monthly newsletter so you don't miss out on any special offers or new releases.

•Links to follow me on Amazon or social media to be kept up to date with new releases.

•Free books and bonus content.

•Opportunities to read my books before they are even released by joining my team.

•Sneak peeks at new material before anyone else.

stellaandrews.com

Follow me on Amazon

Printed in Great Britain
by Amazon

35000958R00148